THE
FLOODS
12

BEWITCHED

THE FLOODS

12

BEWITCHED

Colin Thompson

illustrations by the author

RANDOM HOUSE AUSTRALIA

This work is fictitious. Any resemblance to anyone living or dead is purely coincidental and if you complain about it, you will end up with an invisible friend who pretends to be your friend, but actually gives you bad dreams, bed-wetting and scabby pimples.

A Random House book
Published by Random House Australia Pty Ltd
Level 3, 100 Pacific Highway, North Sydney NSW 2060
www.randomhouse.com.au

First published by Random House Australia in 2013

Addresses for companies within the Random House Group can be found at
www.randomhouse.com.au/offices

National Library of Australia
Cataloguing-in-Publication Entry

Author: Thompson, Colin, (Colin Edward)
Title: Bewitched / Colin Thompson
ISBN: 978 1 74275 530 4 (pbk)
Series: Thompson, Colin (Colin Edward). Floods; 12
Target Audience: For primary school age
Subjects: Witches – Juvenile fiction
         Wizards – Juvenile fiction
         Old age – Juvenile fiction

Design, illustrations and typesetting by Colin Thompson
Additional typesetting by Anna Warren, Warren Ventures Pty Ltd
Printed in Australia by Griffin Press, an accredited ISO AS/NZS 14001:2004 Environmental Management System printer

Random House Australia uses papers that are natural, renewable and recyclable products and made from wood grown in sustainable forests. The logging and manufacturing processes are expected to conform to the environmental regulations of the country of origin.

10 9 8 7 6 5 4 3 2 1

The Floods Family Tree

If you don't know who all the FLOODS are by now, you should be ashamed of yourself.

Of course, you might not have read any of the earlier FLOODS books, in which case you should be double, triple ashamed of yourself for being so useless.

But you can stop being useless by reading ALL the earlier books including the two picture books - THE FLOODS FAMILY FILES and the incredibly brilliant and useful FLOODSOPEDIA.

And then, of course, you will know who EVERYONE is. If, after reading ALL of the FLOODS books, you still don't know who everyone is, crawl into a paper bag and put yourself out with the garbage to get recycled.

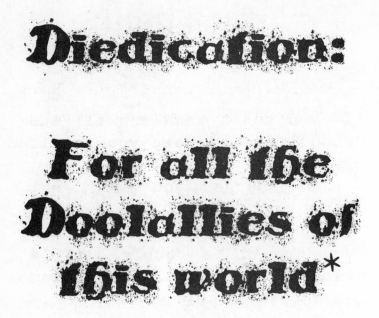

Diedication:

For all the Doolallies of this world*

---

* *You know who you are.*

Prologue

Since *The Floods 11* our hero Nigel Davenport, 39½, has grown a fourth ear on a damp flannel in a jam jar. His other three ears have moved into the jam jar, as they realised it was more exciting there than anywhere on Nigel's body. Of course, this means that Nigel is now totally deaf.

This has two consequences, one bad and one good. The bad one is that he can no longer hear his stunningly gruesome lumpy-skinned seventh wife, Gladys Ferzackerly, when she orders him about. Actually this is a good thing for both of them – for Nigel because he can't hear her constant nagging, and for Gladys because she has never been married to anyone before who didn't keep answering back to her. Another good thing is that it means she hasn't eaten him, like she had her previous seven husbands.

Meanwhile, back in Surreyshire-On-Toast, Nigel's dead mother, Ironica, has been dug up and kidnapped by secret-secret-secret-secret agents

from a wholefood supermarket to be recycled into a delicious organic soup once they have rinsed all the maggots out of her brain.

The future is looking wonderful for Jolyon Whipsnade-Throgmorton, though. Whilst in hospital having a bad infestation of thistle prickles removed from very rude parts of his body, he and the matron, Edith Armature-Tonsil, met and fell in love. They now live in a large wardrobe in the beautiful Scottish Firth of Fifthshire. They are planning to breed something or other, though they can't decide what.

WILL Nigel ever hear again?
WILL Gladys EVER stop nagging and knitting
toilet-seat covers out of barbed wire?
WILL Jolyon and Edith ever be able to domesticate
the Wild Scottish Sporran?

All will be revealed in a very dark room with the lights turned off and under plain wrapper.

But will the wrapper ever make a hit record? Who cares, read this book instead.

'I can't find my socks!'

It was the middle of the night and all through the castle not a creature was stirring, not even a rascal.[1] Nothing, that was, except Nerlin, who was sitting bolt upright in the darkness in a confused panic.

'I can't find my socks and I've gone blind,' he cried.

Mordonna, who had been fast asleep beside him, sat up. 'Sweetheart,' she said, turning on the light, 'you haven't gone blind. It's the middle of the night.'

---

[1] *Which is like a mouse, but rhymes with castle better.*

3

'But I've lost my socks,' Nerlin cried.

'They're on your feet,' said Mordonna.

'Oh,' said Nerlin, lying down again.

Mordonna turned off the light and tried to go back to sleep, but five minutes later, just as she was nodding off . . .

'I've lost my feet!'

'They're on the ends of your legs,' Mordonna mumbled.

'But it's dark. I can't find them.'

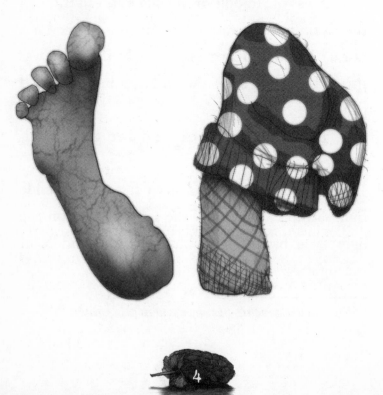

'Do you know where your socks are?' said Mordonna.

'Yes, of course I do. They're at the bottom of the bed.'

'Right. Now reach down and touch them. What can you feel?'

'Feet,' said Nerlin. 'Horrible, cold, clammy feet.'

'Those are your feet.'

'How can you be so sure of that?' said Nerlin. 'It's dark. They don't feel like my feet. I think some subversive revolutionaries might have kidnapped my feet and left these in their place.'

'There are no subversive revolutionaries in Transylvania Waters,' said Mordonna. 'Everybody loves you.'

'The Plank doesn't,' said Nerlin. 'The Plank wants to turn Transylvania Waters into a republic.'

The Plank, or to use his real name, Bert Scroggins, was Transylvania Waters's only property developer. Because everyone thought that things were pretty well perfect as they were, no one actually wanted anything to change. So far, the only property that Bert Scroggins had developed involved replacing a narrow plank across a ditch three miles out of town with a much wider plank and a sign that said *This plank has been placed here for your convenience by the Scroggins Development Corporation.* This was how he had got his nickname. The Plank was not a happy man, but he continued to submit development plans to the Transylvania Waters Development Committee in the hope that they would at least agree to one of his schemes. This was unlikely, as there was no such thing as the Transylvania Waters Development Committee and all his letters were recycled by the Transylvania Waters Department of Recycling, which was actually a goat called Jock.

'No, darling. I've told you this already,' said Mordonna. 'The Plank wants to turn the old Transylvania Waters gasworks into a pub.'

'Oh. Well, those aren't my feet down there in my socks,' said Nerlin. 'In fact, they're not even my socks. They are revolutionary socks fitted with bugging devices and they are transmitting every single word we say.'

'And we've been through that before, haven't we?' said Mordonna. 'Can you remember what I told you?'

'No.'

'I told you that our very clever son, Winchflat, had fitted all your socks with noise-cancelling elastic. Remember?'

Of course Nerlin didn't remember. There were days when he couldn't even remember his own name and insisted he was an eight-year-old girl called Mary. Fortunately, this was not one of those days, but he still insisted his feet belonged to someone else.

'Oh yes, and whose feet are they, then?' Mordonna asked.

'Geoffrey-Geoffrey's.'

Oh no, thought Mordonna, *not Geoffrey-Geoffrey again.*

'I see,' she said. 'So if you've got Geoffrey-Geoffrey's feet, then I expect he's got yours. Now that we know where everyone's feet are, can we please go back to sleep?'

Geoffrey-Geoffrey was Nerlin's new imaginary

friend – not new in the I-used-to-have-an-old-imaginary-friend-and-now-I've-got-a-new-one kind of way, but because this was Nerlin's only imaginary friend. Geoffrey-Geoffrey was new because he had only arrived a few weeks ago after a very heavy marble gargoyle had fallen off a tower in Castle Twilight and bounced off Nerlin's head.[2]

Night-times were becoming more and more like this as Nerlin's mind slowly wandered off to Planet Janet, a lovely happy place where the grass is as blue as the sky, which in Planet Janet is actually pink like sugar candy, and it always feels like spring and the sun shines every single day, except when there's wonderful bright new snow to play in, and your knees, which used to be so knobbly that you won competitions with them, are now as smooth as a princess's cheeks, except when you lose your socks

---

[2] *Actually, Nerlin had had an imaginary friend when he had been about five. He was called Slime Boy and he lived in the ooze that ran down the walls of the drain where the young Nerlin had lived with his downtrodden parents, but Slime Boy had been a false friend and had run away to join the circus. At least that's what Nerlin's mother had told him.*

or your feet or your marbles or something.[3]

And the daytimes were becoming more like this too.

If only my darling husband hadn't refused to eat his broccoli, Mordonna said to herself, *his brain would be as sharp as ever.*

---

[3] *Incredibly, there is actually a planet called Janet, which we will visit sometime in the future, in another time, another place, another galaxy and another series of books. REMEMBER – you heard it here first.*

'Geoffrey-Geoffrey says broccoli is bad for you,' said Nerlin, who had discovered that as he lost the ability to read his own mind, he was developing the ability to read the minds of those around him. 'He says it gives you global warming.'

So she could actually get enough sleep each day, Mordonna had got Nerlin a new special servant.

Bacstairs had been one of Castle Twilight's gardeners, the inventor of the black marigold, which was Transylvania Waters's most popular flower. It was used for weddings and funerals and as a local anaesthetic – a true flower for every occasion. Nerlin and Bacstairs often met each other as the king wandered around the garden and they seemed to get on very well, so he was the obvious choice when Mordonna decided Nerlin needed his own personal manservant.

'The trick is,' said Dr Charles A'tan, Transylvania Waters's top psychiatrist,[4] 'that when someone goes

---

[4] *Dr A'tan was actually Transylvania Waters's ONLY psychiatrist, though, of course, there were also the famous Transylvania Waters Crones, who were usually three times more gaga than any of their*

gaga – or, as we professionals say, Doolally – to provide them with a special caretaker who is more out of it than the patient. That way, the patient thinks they are actually perfectly OK when, in fact, they are barking mad.'

Mordonna wasn't convinced of the doctor's train of thought, but she had to admit that Bacstairs was the perfect candidate for the job. Bacstairs adored King Nerlin and thought of him as a living god.

'My lord,' he said, as he gently removed sixteen daisies from Nerlin's nose with a pair of tweezers,[5] 'I have lost count of the number of times I have dreamed of being your loyal manservant, not once believing it would ever happen.'

---

patients but were experts in the Olde Ways, with herbs and earth and slimy stuff. Pretty much every village in Transylvania Waters had a crone who they went to if they were ill. See the back of this book for a small selection of their treatments.

[5] *Nerlin had been unusually Doolally that day and had become convinced that dark forces were trying to steal all the daisies in Transylvania Waters. Naturally, he thought his nose was the perfect place to hide them.*

'Fourteen,' said Nerlin.

'Fourteen?' said Bacstairs.

'Yes. That's how many times you dreamt of being my whatever it is you just said,' Nerlin explained.

Counting was not a gift Bacstairs had been blessed with. So he hadn't so much lost count as never been able to do it in the first place. Unsurprisingly, he was deeply impressed when his master told him it had been fourteen times, even though the actual figure was close to several thousand.

After Bacstairs had invented the black marigold and totally failed to invent the black rose, his life had never been so exciting again and he found himself thinking cruel and resentful thoughts about innocent things like marigolds and buttercups. So he was only too happy to get out of the garden and spend the rest of his life without Transylvania Waters's earth under his fingernails.[6]

Bacstairs slept in a box outside the royal

---

[6] *Transylvania Waters's earth is not like the earth in other places. It is actually alive and has a rather wicked sense of humour, which I am not allowed to tell you about.*

bedchamber, ready to take care of his beloved lord and master at a moment's notice. It was a very special box, the sort of box that many people dream of sleeping in. Mordonna was beginning to think it would only be a matter of time before Nerlin would have to sleep in a box of his own outside the royal bedchamber so she could get a decent night's sleep.

Mordonna had tried putting Nerlin to bed in one of the grandchildren's nurseries, now that the children had moved on to more grown-up bedrooms.

At first Nerlin had been delighted. There were pretty black witches on broomsticks hanging from the ceiling and they glowed in the dark with a comforting blue light. There were luminous stars and planets and skulls on the ceiling too, and the scent of Friar's Balsam[7] in the air, and the bed had special creaking bones and groaning noises made by

---

[7] *Friar's Balsam is a fragrant resin that comes from the sunny meadows of Sumatra and also comes in a small brown bottle. When I was a little boy and had a stuffed-up cold, my mother would put a few drops in a bowl of hot water and I would inhale it. It was supposed to clear my head. I can't remember if it did, but it smelled nice, just like a sunny meadow in Sumatra.*

a little machine that Winchflat had created for his beloved daughter, Princess Transistor.

But then, Nerlin, who had slept in a huge bed beside his beloved wife for as long as he could remember and quite a few years more than that, had turned over in the new much narrower bed and fallen on the floor. This had made him call for the castle guards to search for the burglars who had had stolen half the bed.

'And I landed on top of Geoffrey-Geoffrey and he got a great big bruise,' said Nerlin.

So now Nerlin was back in the royal bed-chamber again.

'We have to do something about your father,' said Mordonna.

She had gathered the children together in her study, while Bacstairs had taken Nerlin for a walk down to Lake Tarnish to play with the frogspawn.

'How do you mean?' said Betty. 'He seems happier than he's ever been.'

'Yes, I know, but he's losing his grip on reality,' said Mordonna. 'Dr A'tan says he is well on his way to becoming totally Doolally.'

'Do what?' said Merlinmary.

'Doolally,' said Valla. 'It means "away with the fairies".'

'Yes,' Mordonna agreed, 'except that in your

father's case, I tried that, but the fairies refused to take him.'

'But he's happy,' Betty insisted. 'Isn't that the most important thing? I mean, what's wrong with having an invisible friend and talking to flowers? We've all done that, haven't we?'

'Yes, maybe,' said Merlinmary, and everyone else nodded. 'But they don't reply, do they?'

Betty said nothing and did her best to hide her look of surprise. She had several invisible friends and they all replied. She once had an invisible friend called Sultana-Bread, who never stopped talking, and the only way Betty finally managed to shut her up was by eating her.[8]

The other children agreed with Betty. They loved their father, and so what if he did say hello to the grass and the trees every day? It didn't bother anyone.

'It's not as if he actually runs the country,' said

---

[8] *This had nearly put Betty off invisible friends for life because, as everyone knows, currants, raisins and sultanas are gross and disgusting and are like slimy rabbit's poo.*

16

Valla. 'Mother, we all know he's never been the sharpest knife in the box, and that you've looked after everything.'

'But . . .' Mordonna began.

She tried to explain that Nerlin's Doolallyness was ruining her sleep. 'I mean, it's like someone snoring, only worse,' she said. 'And I'm tired all the time.'

'Well, maybe I can come up with an invention,' said Winchflat. 'A special hat or something.'

'Who for?' said Mordonna. 'Me or him?'

'Maybe you could have matching his and hers hats,' said Betty, who was becoming very fashion-conscious as she grew older.

'I don't see how a hat's going to help, unless I roll it up and stuff it in your father's mouth to keep him quiet,' Mordonna snapped. Tiredness was making her short-tempered.

'I'm thinking like those headphones you wear that cut out all the noise around you,' Winchflat explained. 'But I'm assuming, Mother, that you don't want to wear headphones in bed every night.'

'You are always so considerate,' said Mordonna. 'You're absolutely right. Just imagine what big lumpy headphones would do to my hair.'

Winchflat was about to say that he hadn't actually thought about his mother's hair, but more the idea that sleeping with them pushing into the side of one's head all night meant they'd probably slide off. Instead he just nodded. It never did any harm to have Mordonna think you were totally wonderful and caring.

'You would pull the lovely, soft, knitted hat down over your ears – a hat, I might add, that would be designed to enhance your hair and ensure its perfect flatness – and you would firmly but gently press the "on" button and be instantly surrounded by complete silence,' Winchflat said.

'That sounds perfect,' said Mordonna. 'Except for one thing.'

'Which is?'

'If your father had an attack of severe Doolallyness in the middle of the night and I couldn't hear him calling out to me, he'd just start shaking me until I woke up.'

'Well, of course he would,' Winchflat replied in a flash. 'That's why there are two parts to the wonderful Hat of Silence. You would wear the lovely hat, while Father would be pinned to the bed with iron chains, shackles and big lumps of lead.'

Although Nerlin's collapsing brainpower was spoiling the wonderful calmness of her life and sleep, Mordonna loved Nerlin no less than she had the day they had met. So the idea of chaining him down wasn't an option she fancied.

'There must be something else we can do,' she said.

'What about the Old Crones?' said Valla. 'They reckon they can cure anything. They did wonders for me when I got the flu.'

'They cured it?' said Winchflat.

'Goodness me, no,' said Valla. 'They developed it into full-blown bubonic plague. It was wonderful.'

'When I got the flu,' said Satanella, 'the Old Crones didn't give me the plague. All I got was mange and a bottle of smelly shampoo.'

'At least shampoo's better than real poo,' said Merlinmary.

'Well, you would say that, wouldn't you? You're not a dog,' said Satanella.

'Do you remember, Mother, when we came back here and reclaimed the throne?' Valla asked.

'Quenelle the Old Crone gave us shelter in her cave for the night.'[9]

'Indeed I do,' said Mordonna.

'Well, she is the top crone,' Valla explained. 'She's the one the other Old Crones go to when they are unwell.'

'And her bacon sandwiches were among the finest I have ever tasted,' said Mordonna, who was something of an expert in the bacon department.

So it was agreed that before Winchflat created any gadgets, even soft fluffy ones with no padlocks, gags or pointy bits at all, they would take Nerlin up into the mountains to visit Quenelle, Queen of the Old Crones.

---

[9] *See* The Floods 8: Better Homes and Gardens.

'A picnic?' said Nerlin. 'Brilliant. Will we have a campfire and sausages?'

'Yes,' said Mordonna. 'In fact, it's not so much a picnic as a camping holiday.'

'Wow! With tents and everything?'

'Yes, tents, campfires, sausages, and lashings of lemonade,' said Mordonna.

'Wow?' said Nerlin. 'And you know what? This will be Geoffrey-Geoffrey's first picnic ever.'

'How do you know he didn't have lots of picnics before you met him?' said Betty.

'He told me he hadn't,' said Nerlin.

At first Betty had been happy that her father had an invisible friend. She loved her dad and if an

invisible friend made him happy, then it made her happy too. Of course, being a wizard meant that Geoffrey-Geoffrey might not even be imaginary. Unlike humans, whose invisible friends were just part of their imagination, witches and wizards could have all sorts of invisible friends and relations who were only too real. But there was something about Geoffrey-Geoffrey that was suspicious and was beginning to drive Betty crazy.

Actually she was at that awkward age where pretty well everyone, apart from her best friend Ffiona, drove her crazy, but she was beginning to really hate Geoffrey-Geoffrey. He symbolised everything that upset her about her poor father's declining brain. Things like Alzheimer's disease and general Doolallyness weren't supposed to happen to witches and wizards. They were the sorts of things that humans got. In fact, lots of humans seemed to spend their whole lives like that. Betty was starting to wonder if Geoffrey-Geoffrey might have something to do with her darling father's state of mind.

'Betty, stop teasing your father,' Mordonna

23

snapped. 'Things are hard enough as it is, without you stressing him out too.'

'I'm sorry,' said Betty. 'It's just that it's really upsetting to see Dad turning into a vegetable.'

'Geoffrey-Geoffrey says vegetables are good for you,' said Nerlin. 'Except broccoli, of course.'

It took two and a half days to get everyone and everything ready to go up into the mountains. If Nerlin hadn't been going, it would probably only have taken a couple of hours.

First of all they had to go and find some Royal Donkeys, which weren't so much Royal Donkeys as Ex-Royal Donkeys. After Maldegard and Edna had ridden Blossom and Bubbles, the descendants of George-The-Donkey-Formerly-Known-As-Prince-Kevin-Of-Assisi, simply known as George, on their map-making quest, it had been decided to give all the donkeys their freedom.

Now, as everyone knows, Transylvania Waters donkeys have the power of speech, and, like humans, they have a whole range of different personalities. Some are quite bad-tempered on account of not being

24

horses. Some are very happy on account of mysterious and wonderful chemicals in the Transylvania Waters clover and thistles. Once free to roam where they liked, most of them had gone to live in remote little valleys up in the mountains, where the water was clear and sweet, the grass was as soft as velvet and porridge grew in big tasty lumps on enchanted bushes.

It would have taken far too long to go and recruit these donkeys for the expedition to the Old Crones, so it was among the donkeys that had stayed down on the plains or in Dreary itself that they looked for their volunteers. Blossom and Bubbles had actually stayed right in the middle of town and opened a comedy club, where seven nights a week they told their legendary seventeen funny jokes, none of which were rude, not even the one with the knicker elastic in it.

'Go up and visit the Old Crones, you say?' said Blossom.

'Bit of a holiday might be nice,' said Bubbles. 'I say, have you heard the one about the piglet and the chamber-pot?'

Everyone had.

About fifteen thousand times.

'I haven't heard it,' said Nerlin.

About fifteen thousand and one times.

'I don't get it,' said Nerlin. 'Why did the piglet climb inside the chamber-pot in the first place?'

Betty told him to ask Geoffrey-Geoffrey to explain it.

Blossom and Bubbles collected some of the other donkeys that had stayed in town.

The castle's Sandwich Chef made mountains of sandwiches, including grass sandwiches for the donkeys. The castle's Hot Drinks Chef made gallons of hot tea, including Grass Tea for the donkeys and Gravitea for Nerlin to stop him falling off Blossom. The castle's Cake Chef made a seven-metre-long chocolate Transylvania Waters Roll – which is like a Swiss Roll, only longer and with lots more chocolate – and finally the castle's Lolly Chef gave everyone[10] a paper bag of lollies with absolutely no

---

[10] *Yes, yes, including the donkeys.*

liquorice at all, though there was a warning notice
printed on each bag to say that the lollies may have
been in the same castle as some peanuts.[11]

---

[11] *See the back of the book for an incomplete list of Castle
Twilight Chefs.*

The castle's Clothes Chef gave everyone[12] a warm scarf. The donkeys mistook theirs for snacks and promptly ate them.

So, finally, they were ready to set off.

Except Nerlin.

'No, I can't go,' he said.

'What is it now, my darling?' said Mordonna.

'Someone has stolen my bottom,' said Nerlin.

'You've got your trousers on back to front again,' said Mordonna.

Then they were finally, finally ready to go.

'Where is Geoffrey-Geoffrey's donkey?' said Nerlin.

'I thought he could just ride on Blossom with you,' said Mordonna.

'I think the two of us would be too heavy for one donkey.'

'No, you wouldn't,' said Blossom, who knew all about Geoffrey-Geoffrey and had actually had an invisible friend of her own when she had been

_____

[12] *See footnote 10.*

28

younger. 'Before Tubby-Tubby ran away to join the Belgian Foreign Legion[13] she used to ride everywhere on my back.'

Then they were finally, finally, finally ready to go. Except . . .

'There is NO except,' Mordonna snapped, as she climbed onto Bubbles' back and led everyone out of the castle gate onto the street.

'Which road leads out of town?' she asked Bubbles.

'All of them,' said Bubbles, an answer which, of course, was perfectly true but not much help.

A crowd of three people and a dachshund called Sir Frances Treves – named after Sir Frances Treves[14] – cheered as the party passed and then went and collected their cheering fee from the castle office.

What with Nerlin wanting to stop and say

---

[13] *Which is like the French Foreign Legion, except that it's not French, is only open to invisible donkeys and doesn't actually exist except as a lie that Tubby-Tubby had told Blossom to hide the embarrassing fact that she was going to take part in* Australia's Got Talent.

[14] *Whoever he was.*

hello to everyone they passed, especially Sir Frances Treves, it was getting dark by the time they reached the edge of town.[15] So they went back to the castle for a good night's sleep before setting off at the crack of dawn the next day in the hope of reaching Quenelle's cave by nightfall.

---

[15] *And Dreary was a very small town.*

On their way up the mountain the next day, Nerlin greeted every tree they passed, all seven hundred and thirty-two of them. Fortunately, he did not insist on stopping to do this. He also said hello to the grass and the sky, seventy-two butterflies, a family of bow-legged goats and a partridge quite near a pear tree. Fortunately, none of them greeted him back, apart from one of the goats, which tried to eat his sock as he rode by.

'Tell me,' Nerlin said to his daughter-in-law Maldegard – Transylvania Waters's official map-maker – as they rode along side by side,[16] 'did you

---

[16] *Mordonna had decided that everyone in the travelling party had to take turns riding side by side with Nerlin.*

come up here when you were making the *Great Transylvania Waters Atlas*?'

Now, Maldegard had a kind and gentle disposition and although she admitted Nerlin's brain was becoming a bit erratic as he got older, she refused to accept that he was going Doolally or even had a problem.

'He's just a bit eccentric,' she'd said earlier to her husband, Winchflat. 'And who can blame him, what with his age and having the responsibility of running an entire country?'

Winchflat had pointed out that it was actually Mordonna who ran things and the only responsibility that Nerlin had to deal with was deciding what colour sprinkles to have on his cereal each morning.

'Let's face, it my darling – Papa is losing it,' he'd said.

'Losing what?' Maldegard had protested. 'I would say that as time goes by, he gets happier and happier.'

'Yes, but what about the rest of us who have to live with it?' said Winchflat.

'That's your problem,' Maldegard said. 'I think it's much more important to be happy than to remember how to tie your shoelaces.'

'Yes, but –'

'But nothing. You're all just being selfish, and anyway he is the King and everyone loves him. There are plenty of people who are only too happy to tie his shoelaces for him.'

And, really, Maldegard was right. She said that

as Nerlin got older and his brain started to shrink, all he was doing was clearing out the stuff he didn't need anymore. She said, and honestly no one could argue with her, that the world would be a far better place if more people had invisible friends and went around saying good morning to bushes instead of running around shooting and fighting each other.

'Yes, we did come up here when we were making the maps,' she lied to Nerlin. 'And you'll never guess what we called this lovely little valley that we're travelling up now.'

'What? What?' said Nerlin with the eagerness of a four-year-old child.

'We called this place Geoffrey-Geoffrey Shire.'

Nerlin was ecstatic. 'Wow,' he said.

'And the whole area, the three hills over there and the other nearby valleys are called The Land of Invisible Friends,' Maldegard continued.

'No!' said Nerlin, looking around with his eyes wide open and a huge happy smile on his face. 'So do you think there are lots of other invisible friends living up here?'

'I'm sure there are.'

'And I suppose they're all waiting for a visible friend to come along and find them, like I did with Geoffrey-Geoffrey,' said Nerlin. 'Except I was back at home having a bath when Geoffrey-Geoffrey appeared.'

'Right,' said Maldegard. 'Though I expect here is where he grew up.'

'Yes, I expect it was,' said Nerlin. 'After all, you can't just have invisible friends wandering around the countryside tripping people up and bumping into things. It's obvious they'd all have to live in the same place until they found their visible friend.'

'Exactly,' said Maldegard.

'I wonder why Geoffrey-Geoffrey came up out of the plughole.'

Maldegard was nothing if not quick-thinking and very imaginative.

'Oh, that's easy to explain,' she said. 'The purest water in the whole of Transylvania Waters is in this stream we're travelling by, so I imagine this water is used in the King's bathtub at Castle Twilight.'

'Yes, of course,' Nerlin agreed. 'So Geoffrey-Geoffrey must have fallen in the water and got carried all the way down to my bathroom.'

'That's right,' said Maldegard.

'What a fantastic bit of luck,' said Nerlin. 'I mean, just suppose it had been someone else having a bath that night. Geoffrey-Geoffrey would be their invisible friend and not mine.'

'Yes,' said Maldegard, 'and as we know, not everyone is as friendly to invisible friends as you are. So it wasn't just lucky for you, but it was lucky for Geoffrey-Geoffrey too.'

Overhearing their conversation, Mordonna decided that Maldegard would now be the one and only Official-Side-By-Side-With-The-King-Rider, which everyone was very happy with, apart from Bacstairs, who had got locked in the lavatory back at Castle Twilight by accident,[17] just before the party had set off.

The sun had come up over the mountains and

---

[17] *Or was it? Ooeerrr!*

36

was now making everything in the valley appear warm and golden. The group turned away from the stream and began to climb a steep path to higher ground, where the Old Crones lived.

They could see brightly coloured rags flapping in the distance. These were like the Buddhist prayer flags from the Himalayas, except they weren't prayer flags and they weren't from the Himalayas. They were actually the Old Crones' baggy knickers because it was Friday, which was laundry day. Nevertheless, they were a welcome sight, telling the party they were on the right path.

They reached a small plateau of the softest green grass and instantly every single donkey began drooling. This wonderful grass was not there by accident. It was an early-warning device planted by the Old Crones to alert them of approaching donkeys.

The Old Crones knew that as soon as any donkey saw the grass they would have to stop and eat it, which would give the Old Crones time to take any action they needed. Why they wanted to

be warned of approaching donkeys is not quite clear, though a few years earlier there had been a plague of salesmen bothering people everywhere as they tried to sell them a really rubbish set of encyclopedias,[18] and they had travelled by donkey.[19]

'Time for lunch,' said Bubbles, stopping in her tracks and refusing to move another step.

'Yeah, time for lunch,' all the other donkeys agreed.

'Hooray,' cried Nerlin. 'Picnic time.'

The Picnic Blanket Maid spread the picnic blankets on the grass and the Picnic Maid laid the food out and the Picnic Beverages Maid poured out the drinks. Nerlin, not realising that there were

---

[18] *See the back of the book for some information about these useless reference books.*

[19] *They were NOT Transylvania Waters donkeys but a really cheap herd of Belgian donkeys, and you could actually get one free if you bought the encyclopaedias. Luckily, very few of these were sold and the salesmen, their encyclopaedias and their donkeys were hounded out of the country by a pack of Wilfhounds, which sound like wolfhounds but are actually snappy little terriers all called Wilf.*

separate picnics for the wizards and the donkeys, began wolfing down grass sandwiches.

'These sandwiches taste just like grass,' he said.

'Yes, well, Father . . .' Winchflat began.

'They're absolutely brilliant!' Nerlin cried.

'They're actually meant for the donkeys,' said Mordonna.

'Oh, don't be silly,' said Nerlin. 'They're much too good for donkeys. They'd rather eat grass. Oh, this is grass. Umm, sorry about that.'

At this point, most people would have spat out what they had in their mouth. Nerlin didn't and, when no one was looking, he took another sandwich.

'Note to self,' he said, 'replace cucumber sandwiches with grass ones for afternoon tea.'

'No problem, Your Majesty,' said Blossom. 'You eat as many as you like. We'll make do with this field.'

'And help yourself to the Grass Tea too,' said Bubbles. 'We'll just drink this crystal-clear pure water from the stream.'

'There's Grass Tea too?' said Nerlin. 'Brilliant!'

He picked up a bucket of the donkeys' tea and drained it.

'Yuck, that's revolting,' he said. 'It tastes just like grass.'

'Here, Father, have a strawberry-jam sandwich,' said Betty.

'Oh yes, that's delicious,' said Nerlin. 'Though I think the grass ones have the edge.'

So, like most things going on round Nerlin, the picnic was eccentric chaos, but pretty well everyone was happy, except Blossom's cousin Muriel, who was always miserable. When everyone asked her why, she said she wasn't so much miserable as performing a tribute.

'It's a homage to the most famous donkey in the whole world,' she said. 'Eeyore from *Winnie the Pooh*. He's my ultimate hero and he was always miserable.'

'So it makes you feel happy and fulfilled being miserable?' Blossom asked.

'Yes, it does.'

'So you're happy being miserable, which means that, actually, you are the opposite of Eeyore,' said Bubbles.

'Damn,' said Muriel. 'Now I'm really miserable.'

'Listen, you donkeys,' Mordonna called out, 'if you don't stop doing philosophy, I'll turn you into poodles.'

'That would be better than being miserable,' said Muriel.

'Belgian poodles,' said Mordonna. 'With dandruff.'

That made the donkeys talk about football, which has no philosophical content whatsoever. A sub-group of donkeys decided they'd rather talk about cricket, but they all fell asleep, because that's what cricket does to people.

'If we don't get a move on,' said Valla, 'it'll be dark before we get to the caves.'

'I thought we were going to camp out under the stars,' said Nerlin.

'No, sweetheart, the plan is to camp in, not out,' said Mordonna. 'We will camp inside the Old

Crones' guest caves and sleep in the finest feather beds.'

'With our sleeping bags?' said Nerlin.

'If you want to,' said Mordonna.

It had been a long day and it was getting longer. Mordonna felt like slipping away, back down the mountain to the castle and into her own bed, but she climbed onto Bubbles' back and the party continued on their journey up to the caves.

'Halt, who goes there?' said a voice from behind a bush.

'We do,' said Nerlin.

'I know that voice,' said Betty.

'I know that voice,' said the voice.

'I know those voices,' said a second voice from behind another bush.

'What are you two doing here?' said yet another voice from behind a completely different bush.

'Just you come out here this minute,' said Betty. 'All of you.'

Three middle-aged women badly disguised as little old ladies badly disguised as bushes came out from behind their three real bushes. It was the

three ex-peasants who had helped Betty and Ffiona by pretending to be three cookery witches.[20] Since then they had moved up in the world. They had also moved down, sideways and backwards, as well as forwards, though not at the same time.

'Oh look, Mother,' Betty said. 'It's the three wonderful Cookery Witches.'

'Yeah, right,' said Mordonna, who knew perfectly well that they were fake cooks, but couldn't quite prove it. 'I see they have moved up in the world by becoming fake bushes.'

'Exactly,' said Fake Cook One aka Fake Bush One.

'Indeed,' said Fake Bush Two. 'We now has regular employment.'

'Yes,' said Fake Bush Three, 'we is working for the Old Crones as their security guards.'

'Well, you go and tell your employers that their King and Queen are here and want to see them,' said Mordonna.

---

[20] *See* The Floods 11: Disasterchef.

44

'No need, Your Majesty,' said Fake Bush One. 'They already know all that and they said to make you welcome and escort you up to the caves.'

'OK,' said Mordonna. 'Lead on.'

'We has to make you welcome first, Your Majesty,' said Fake Bush Two.

The three Fake Bushes prostrated themselves on the ground but instead of saying 'Oh most Glorious Majesties, we welcome you to the Caves of the Old Crones,' all they could do was cry out in pain and say 'Ow, OW, OWWW!'

'What is the matter with you?' said Mordonna.

'Sharp bushes. Oww,' Fake Bush One cried.

'We needs pruning,' said Fake Bush Two.

'You haven't got any secateurs, have you?' said Fake Bush One. Fake Bush Three was in so much pain she couldn't speak.

'Are those acacia bushes?' said Blossom.

They were, and when Fake Bush One said so, the Floods backed away in horror, because, as everyone knows, witches and wizards are terrified

45

of acacia trees (and bushes).[21] This, of course, was why the Old Crones had used them to disguise their security guards and had them growing everywhere.

'Donkeys love acacia,' said Bubbles. 'We will eat you out of your agony.'

'Is it just me, or has everyone else noticed that those bushes are talking to us?' said Nerlin.

'They are not bushes, my darling,' said Mordonna. 'They are people.'

'I think your mother is losing it,' Nerlin whispered to Betty. 'She thinks those talking bushes are people.'

'They are, Father,' said Betty.

'Yes, she's right,' said Winchflat, who had been near enough to catch the whisper.

OMG, Nerlin thought, *I seem to be the only one in the family who hasn't been infected with Doolallyness.*

---

[21] *Readers of earlier Floods books will already know this, as it was the very reason the Floods had chosen to live in Acacia Avenue – which, by the way, had been a totally acacia-free street – to try to keep the agents of Mordonna's father, the evil King Quatorze, away. See every Floods book ever written and any others not yet written or published.*

After a huge amount of 'Ouches', 'Ahhhs' and 'Ooohs' plus a few 'Ow, that is not part of a bush', followed by lots of ointment and cups of strong sweet tea, the three middle-aged women disguised as little old ladies were finally free and ready to officially greet the visitors and lead them up to the caves.

Except that the donkeys, who were full up with acacia, all wanted to lie down and have a sleep.

'Everyone knows it's really bad to go mountain-climbing straight after a meal,' said Blossom. 'You can get terrible stomach cramps.'

'And wind,' said Bubbles. 'Actually, you get lots of wind after acacia, even if you stand perfectly still.'

And by now it was dark and no one had a torch. So there was another delay while one of the middle-aged women rode up to the caves on the donkey that could see really well in the dark on account of a Night-Vision Spell that Mordonna had cast on him, on a mission to find a torch.

'I wish you'd done an Anti-Wind Spell as well, Mother,' said Betty, as the donkey went off into the darkness followed by an endless trail of leaky explosions.

'Good idea,' said Mordonna, clicking her fingers, but all the spell did was make the explosions silent, which didn't really help a lot. The smell and the clouds of green smoke were still there.

By the time the donkey came back with the torch and everyone had finally reached the caves, it was long past dinner time. The smell of the finest grilled bacon drifting down the path only made things worse. Or, rather, it would have done if it hadn't been for the donkey-acacia wind that had mingled with it and turned it into a smell that put most people off any thought of food.

48

'Wow, what is that smell?' said Nerlin, who unsurprisingly thought it was amazing. 'It's like the wonderful smell of bacon, only fifty times better.'

Two of the less important Old Crones led the donkeys away downwind from the caves, so by the time they got into the cave and sat down, all they could smell was the perfect unadulterated scent of the bacon itself.[22]

Quenelle, the Queen of the Old Crones, made it perfectly clear that eating bacon sandwiches was far more important than anything anyone could ever say, so she said nothing until everyone was on their third sandwich.

'You are all most welcome,' she said as everyone wiped the bacon fat off their chins with their sleeves.[23] 'And as the ancient philosophers of

---

[22] *Which, as everyone knows, is one of the three most perfect smells in the world. The second greatest smell is bacon and the third is more bacon. And, as I sit here writing this, I am beginning to drool and want bacon, and, hey, it's nearly lunch time!*

[23] *Apart from King Nerlin and Queen Mordonna, who were each given a handmaiden's sleeve to use.*

Atlantis discovered, there is nothing quite like bacon to help the brain to focus. Bit of a pity that, because the island of Atlantis was underwater, so the scent of bacon floated out through the waves, attracting the biggest gathering of sharks ever recorded, and once the bacon had gone the sharks ate the Atlanteans, which is how their whole civilisation was wiped out. However, we are up a tall mountain, which is a shark-free zone. So sleep well, for tomorrow we will untangle our beloved King's Doolally brain.'

That night, because the bacon they'd eaten had been enchanted bacon, everyone had the most wonderful dreams, and the next morning they awoke feeling very peaceful.

While everyone else did a lot of rambling and wandering around among and in between the mountains, Quenelle and her two top Old Crones sat down with Nerlin to assess the situation.

'How many fingers am I holding up?' Quenelle said, raising her hand in the air.

'You are not holding up any of them,' said Nerlin. 'They are standing up themselves on the top of your hand.'

'And who is the prime minister of Transylvania

Waters?' said Anorexya, the second Old Crone.

'I am,' said Nerlin.

'What does two and two make?' asked Dispepsya, the third Old Crone.

'That depends entirely on which four you are talking about,' Nerlin replied.

'Stick out your tongue,' said Quenelle.

'I can't do that,' said Nerlin. 'My mum always said it was rude to poke out your tongue.'

'No, this is all right,' Quenelle explained. 'It's for medical reasons. I need to examine it.'

Nerlin looked down at his chest and began muttering to himself.

'Are you talking to Geoffrey-Geoffrey?' said Dispepsya.

'Yes, I am,' said Nerlin. 'How did you know?'

'Well,' said Quenelle, 'surely you don't think that Geoffrey-Geoffrey has only got one friend in the whole world, do you? Can you imagine how lonely he would be?'

'I never thought of that,' said Nerlin. 'But he's my special friend.'

'Of course he is,' the three Old Crones agreed. 'But we are his friends, too. You don't imagine he got as clever as he is without some help, do you?'

Nerlin didn't.

'That's why all the invisible friends live in that valley you came through on your way here – they come up here every day for cleverness lessons,' Quenelle explained.

'My family doesn't think Geoffrey-Geoffrey is real,' said Nerlin. 'They don't believe in him.'

'Well, maybe they should come here for lessons too.'

'Yes, I'll tell them to,' Nerlin agreed.

'Actually, no. It's probably not a good idea,' said Quenelle. 'In fact, I think we should keep the invisible friends stuff to ourselves.'

'Anyway, now that you've had a chat with Geoffrey-Geoffrey, will you let me look at your tongue?' she continued.

'Yes, OK then. Geoffrey-Geoffrey said I should.'

'Of course he did,' said Anorexya. 'We all know what a clever boy Geoffrey-Geoffrey is, don't we?'

Nerlin nodded and poked out his tongue.

Looks of horror spread across the three Old Crones' faces. They told Nerlin to put his tongue away and wait while they went off into the corner and whispered to each other.

'It is the map?' Nerlin said.

'You know about the map?' said Quenelle.

'Of course I do,' said Nerlin. 'I see it every time I look in the mirror.'

'What, you mean you poke your tongue out every time you look in the mirror?' said Anorexya.

'Of course not. Mummy told me it was rude,' said Nerlin. 'So I only do it in the mornings when I'm shaving.'

'Shaving?'

'Yes. There's nothing worse than having a hairy tongue,' Nerlin explained. 'If you have scrambled eggs for breakfast, you end up with bits stuck in your mouth hair all day.'

'Yes, but the map,' Anorexya said.

'Yes, it's Transylvania Waters,' said Nerlin. 'It's a special birthmark that all the kings of our wonderful

country have. Prince Valla, my eldest son, who will be king one day, has got one too. Winchflat, who would be next in line, has a very faint outline of it.'

'But it's not of Transylvania Waters,' said Quenelle.

'Yes it is,' said Nerlin.

'No it's not,' said Dispepsya. 'Wait here, we'll get a mirror and show you.'

'It hasn't turned into Belgium, has it?' said Nerlin. 'Please tell me it's not Belgium.'

'It's not Belgium,' said Quenelle. 'You say that as though it's happened before.'

'Not really,' said Nerlin. 'I had a nightmare once where that did happen and all my toes turned into turnips.'

It turned out that it had happened when Nerlin had eaten a very, very large piece of vintage gorgonzola – a variety of cheese made with real gorgons – just before going to bed.[24]

---

[24] *There really is a type of cheese called gorgonzola. It isn't actually made with gorgons but it does smell that way. As I was writing this book, I thought I should do some research. So I ate*

'No, Your Majesty. It is not a map of Belgium,' said Quenelle.

'It's not a map of Rockall, where my beloved wife's awful father was banished to, is it?'[25]

'No, Your Majesty. It is not a map of Rockall.'

'Thank goodness,' said Nerlin. 'So, what is it?'

'Well, there's good news and there's bad news,' said Quenelle.

'Yes?'

'The good news is that it's a place a long, long way away.'

'And the bad news?'

'The only connection we can find with this place is that deep in its surrounding waters there is a bottle in which your arch-enemy, the Hearse Whisperer, was once trapped,' Quenelle explained. 'The bottle's been empty for a while, and besides, now that you are the King of Transylvania Waters,

---

a large piece of this cheese at bedtime, and I did have a similar dream where my tongue had a map of a tongue that belonged to someone else on it and all my toes turned inside out.

[25] *See* The Floods 8: Better Homes and Gardens.

the Hearse Whisperer should actually be your devoted servant now.'

'So what is the map of?' snapped Nerlin.

'It's a small island off the island of Tristan da Cunha called Inaccessible Island.'

'And what does all this mean?' said Nerlin. 'I've never been anywhere near the place.'

'I don't know,' said Quenelle.

None of them did, not just Anorexya and Dispepsya, but none of the other ten Old Crones either.[26] There was lots of speculation, including:

- *Had Nerlin's ear wax been used to seal the cork of the bottle the Hearse Whisperer had been imprisoned in? (It hadn't.)*
- *Had a long-distance magpie taken some of Nerlin's toenail clippings back to its nest on Inaccessible Island? (It hadn't, though the magpie had sold some of them on eBay, so maybe they could have ended up on the island, except they hadn't.)*

---

[26] *There were always thirteen Old Crones. If one of them died, then another was found. By the way, Old Crones die in a very unique way. They shrivel up like an old leaf, getting smaller and smaller. Then they are laid out on the Shrinking Stone while the remaining twelve Old Crones summon the Winds of Time to take the shrivelled-up body high into the upper atmosphere, where it is carried round the planet in jet streams that go faster and faster until the body is flung out into space always at exactly the same speed and angle so that eventually it comes to land on a planet far, far away, where it is reincarnated as an immortal newsagent, forever wondering if this is all there is.*

- *Had there been some ancient historic relic from Inaccessible Island that had ended up in the Dreary Museum Of Ancient Historic Relics From Very Remote Islands? (There hadn't.)*
- *Had Nerlin lost one of his thongs[27] when the family had been on holiday to Port Folio[28] and had it floated around in the sea for several years before washing up on the beaches of Inaccessible Island? (It hadn't because there are no beaches there. If there were, it would be called Accessible Island.)*
- *All of the above.*
- *None of the above.*
- *Something to do with bacon.[29]*

Although no one knew why the map had changed from Transylvania Waters into this tiny remote uninhabited island, Quenelle was certain of one thing.

---

[27] *THONGS as in Australian shoe – not tiny British knickers.*
[28] *See* The Floods 6: The Great Outdoors.
[29] *As seen in the famous movie* Seven Rashers of Separation.

'Well,' she said, 'I am certain of one thing.'

'And is that one thing in some way connected to our beloved King's tongue map?' said Anorexya.

'It is indeed,' said Quenelle. 'It is my belief that the King has been infected with a virus.

'And if that is the case, Your Majesty,' Quenelle continued, 'it means that you are completely Doolally-free.'

'What about my family?' said Nerlin. 'On our way up here they were having conversations with bushes.'

'That was just a case of mistaken identity,' said Quenelle. 'After all, who among us can say they have never spoken to a bush?'

'Yes, but these bushes answered back,' said Nerlin.

'Well, we've all been there too, haven't we?' said Anorexya.

'I haven't,' said Nerlin. 'Though when I was a little boy living back in the drains, my best friend – well, my only friend, actually – was a patch of green slime that lived on the wall of our tunnel. I used to

talk to him for hours but he never spoke back. My mother called him Slime Boy and said the reason he didn't speak to me was because he had been struck dumb by an evil spell.'

'Same thing,' said Dispepsya.

'I loved Slime Boy,' said Nerlin. 'I really missed him when he went away.'

'What, you saw him go?' Dispepsya asked.

'No, my mother said he had run away to join the circus and it wasn't until years later that I discovered that she'd got rid of him with a scrubbing brush dipped in bleach. I never forgave her for that.'

'Are you sure our great ruler is Doolally-free?' Anorexya whispered to Quenelle.

'Yes, well, maybe not completely,' said Quenelle. 'But I definitely think he's got a virus, which, of course, means one thing.'

'We have to send him to Gruinard,' said Anorexya.

'Yes, she is the only one who can decontaminate him,' Quenelle agreed.

61

'Please don't make me take him,' said Dispepsya. 'My hair still hasn't grown back from last time.'

'We'll draw lots. Gather the others and put everyone's name in a hat,' said Quenelle.

'Not your hat,' said Dispepsya. 'We all know about the remote control.'

Quenelle looked annoyed. She had no choice but to agree to the obvious and fair choice – Nerlin's own hat. Nerlin wasn't too sure about this, but when Quenelle told him it was a draw to raise funds for orphaned semicolons, he agreed.

'And I want to do the draw,' said Dispepsya. 'Since I went last time – and I've got the teeth marks to prove it – I think it's only fair that I should make the draw.'

The other twelve Old Crones gathered round while Dispepsya put her hand into the mysterious darkness that was the inside of Nerlin's hat.

'Mind Dorothy,' said Nerlin.

'Dorothy?'

'Dorothy, my pet rat,' Nerlin explained. 'He's very rare, an endangered species.'

'Rats aren't endangered,' said Quenelle. 'The nasty, verminous things are everywhere.'

'Especially in our dinner,' said Anorexya. 'Nasty yes, verminous yes, but totally delicious too.'

Everyone agreed.

'Dorothy is not dinner,' said Nerlin. 'He is one of only fourteen known living Tristan da Cunha Clucking Rats.'

'Clucking rats?' said Anorexya. 'Are you telling us that they cluck like chickens?'

'Yes,' said Nerlin.

'Next you'll be saying she lays eggs too,' said Quenelle.

'Dorothy is a boy,' said Nerlin. 'Of course he doesn't lay eggs.'

'I think your diagnosis that our glorious leader is not Doolally,' Anorexya whispered to Quenelle, 'is a bit wide of the mark. He's as hopping mad as a kangaroo in a hot frying pan.'

Quenelle missed the last six words because a very loud cock-a-doodle-doo came from deep inside Nerlin's hat, followed by a small golden rat clutching a pawful of torn bits of paper.

After Dorothy had been put to bed in one of Nerlin's pockets, the thirteen Old Crones wrote their names on bits of paper again and put them back in

the hat. Then Dispepsya drew one out.

'I don't believe it,' she said, and banged her hand on her forehead. 'It's not fair.'

'Well, look at it this way,' said Quenelle. 'At least you know the way there.'

'Go where?' said Mordonna, who had been keeping out of the way while the Old Crones tried to analyse Nerlin.

'To visit Gruinard,' said Quenelle. 'Your husband has a viral infection and she is the only witch who can cure him.'

'You mean, all he's got is a viral infection?' said Mordonna. 'He's not going Doolally?'

'I wouldn't go that far,' said Quenelle. 'But first things first. We need to cure the infection and then we can check the Doolallyness. And then, of course, there's the map on his tongue.'

'All the kings of Transylvania Waters have our country map on their tongues,' said Mordonna. 'It's a hereditary royal birthmark.'

'Yes, but, your husband's . . . oh my God . . . the rat!'

'Dorothy?' said Mordonna. 'My beloved adores that rat.'

'Yes, yes, I know,' said Quenelle. 'But where did he say it comes from?'

'It's an endangered Tristan da Cunha Clucking Rat,' said Mordonna.

'Yes, yes, and the map on your husband's tongue is of Inaccessible Island – one of the Tristan da Cunha group of islands!' said Quenelle. 'We need to get Dorothy immediately. Your husband could be in grave danger, and when I say grave, I mean hole in the ground where dead bodies go. I can't believe I didn't pick it up earlier.'

'That won't be so easy,' said Mordonna. 'He won't let anyone touch Dorothy.'

'Your Majesty,' said Quenelle, 'does Dorothy have an invisible friend?'

'What? How can I do that?' said Nerlin. 'He's a rat. Rats can't talk.'

'Well, that's not strictly true,' said Quenelle. 'We have a special potion that can give any animal the power of speech.'

'You do not,' said Nerlin.

'And what about the Transylvania Waters donkeys?' said Quenelle. 'Surely you don't think that their ability to speak was part of natural evolution, do you?'

'I hadn't actually thought about it.'

'Well, it wasn't like that,' Quenelle lied. 'We gave them the power of speech and we could do the same for Dorothy.'

'Really?' said Nerlin doubtfully.

'Just imagine the hours of fun you could have together if he could talk,' said Dispepsya. 'And if Dorothy hasn't got an invisible friend, we could soon get him one.'

'You could?'

'Oh yes,' Quenelle said. 'We are in charge of all the invisible friends in Transylvania Waters.

As you know, they live just below here.'

'We can even make them visible,' said Dispepsya.

'Ooh, I'm not sure about that,' said Nerlin. 'I mean, if I saw what Geoffrey-Geoffrey looked like in real life rather than how I see him now, I might not like him. And I'm not sure I want Dorothy to have an invisible friend. He might want to spend all his time with them instead of me.'

'That's true,' said Quenelle. 'So why don't we just give him the power of speech and forget about the invisible friends bit?'

'You know how much you and Dorothy love it when you push him round in that toy truck?' added Mordonna. 'Well, if Dorothy could speak, you could play toy trains together and Dorothy could be the engine driver.'

'Brilliant!' said Nerlin, and reached into his pocket for the sleeping rat.

Except the rat wasn't sleeping. And although no one knew it but the Old Crones suspected it, Dorothy was not actually a rat, and he had been listening to every word of their conversation.

As Nerlin's open hand approached, Dorothy lunged forward and sank his teeth into it. Nerlin screamed in pain and pulled his hand out with Dorothy still attached to it. Once out in the open the rat let go, but the Old Crones were ready and, before the creature could escape, they threw him into a small cage and locked it.

'You are so going to regret that,' said Dorothy in a weird, evil clockwork-like voice that was far too big to have come out of a medium-sized rat.

'I've just been checking on the net,' said Winchflat, coming into the cave, 'and there's no such creature as a Tristan da Cunha Clucking Rat.'

'Yes there is,' Dorothy growled. 'I'm one.'

'No you're not,' said Winchflat. 'The only rat I can find on Tristan da Cunha is the Clicking Rat.'

'Clicking rat, clucking rat,' Dorothy snapped. 'What's the difference? I'm one of them.'

'And,' Winchflat continued, 'they became extinct fifteen hundred years ago and there are no records of them having been able to speak.'

'No, yes, but that's not strictly true,' Dorothy blustered. 'Extinct on the main island, but there is a small colony of us still living on Inaccessible Island. Um, er, that's why I changed Nerlin's tongue map to there, to remind me of home.'

Dorothy tried to bluff his way out of the situation with no success. He could explain neither why nor how he had left the incredibly remote island and ended up living in Nerlin's hat.

'I was kidnapped by a seagull,' he said, which no one believed for a second.

'I signed on as a cabin boy and finally jumped ship,' he tried. This was even more unbelievable.

'I got stuck in a bottle that had washed up on the beach and then got carried away on the next high tide and over a year later, during which time I had had nothing to eat but plankton and krill, I came ashore in France, where the bottle was found by a bottle collector who couldn't see me inside because of all the green slime that had grown there and when he poked his finger into the bottle and I bit it, he screamed in pain and dropped the bottle on the floor where it shattered, allowing me to escape and jump onto a passing truck on its way to Switzerland, where I was grabbed by a golden eagle who flew here and dropped me in her nest for her children to eat, but I managed to bite both her children before they could bite me and I scrambled down the rocks to safety, which happened to be the back garden of Castle Twilight, where I met King Nerlin,' he said finally.

But no one believed that either, though it was completely true apart from the bits that weren't.

It was agreed that while Dispepsya took Nerlin to visit Gruinard, Winchflat would take Dorothy back to the castle to try and find out exactly what the creature was.

'I will put its brain in my Brain-Washing-Machine and see what we can filter out of the dirty water,' Winchflat said.

This threat finally got through to Dorothy, who began to shake and whimper.

'OK, I'll tell you the truth,' he said. 'My real name is Dorlock.'

'Yes,' said Quenelle. 'Go on.'

'Go on what?' said Dorlock.

'You said you were going to tell us the truth,' said Quenelle. 'So get on with it.'

'I just did,' said the rat. 'My name is Dorlock.'

'And the rest?'

'What rest?'

'The truth,' Quenelle said, and turned to Anorexya. 'If we put the rat in this cage and then place it in a very tall bucket of water, do you think it would sink or float?'

'I don't know,' said Anorexya. 'Let's find out.'

Dorlock wet himself and shivered pathetically.[30]

'Take him away,' said Quenelle to Winchflat.

---

[30] *Don't feel sorry for him. He's a nasty piece of work who wants to destroy the Floods.*

The next morning, after lots of bacon and a few token green things followed by a good night's sleep and some bacon, everyone got ready to go back down to Castle Twilight. Everyone except Dispepsya and Nerlin, who had to travel even higher into the mountains to visit the legendary Virus Witch Gruinard and her Seven Acolytes, who were like trainee Old Crones in that they were neither old nor crones, but made the tea and did the washing up.

'Come on, Your Majesty,' said Dispepsya. 'We must be on our way if we are to reach our destination before nightfall. We have many miles and quite a few kilometres to travel.'

'I'll tell Geoffrey-Geoffrey to get ready,' said Nerlin.

'Oh no, Your Majesty,' said Dispepsya. 'I'm afraid no invisible friends can come with us.'

'But . . .' Nerlin began.

'No, sire, it would end in tears,' Dispepsya explained. 'Gruinard hates almost everything in the whole world, but the one thing she hates more than anything else, apart from Vegemite, of course, are invisible friends. Were Geoffrey-Geoffrey to come with us, he would actually become visible for a few agonising moments as Gruinard engulfed him in a ball of flames.'

Nerlin said that he wasn't sure he actually wanted to meet Gruinard and, just in case there was to be any flame-engulfing, he changed into a pair of flame-proof underpants, which made a really annoying creaking noise for the rest of their trip. It was so annoying that Dispepsya found herself wishing that her beloved King would drop dead.

'I am leaving my own invisible friend here,' said Dispepsya. 'In fact, Fifi-Fifi can keep Geoffrey-

Geoffrey company while we are away.'

That made Nerlin feel a bit better. He was about to say, 'Supposing Geoffrey-Geoffrey and Fifi-Fifi fell in love with each other and wouldn't want to have anything to do with us anymore?' when Dispepsya said:

'Maybe they will fall in love with each other and have lots of wonderful, invisible babies. After all, Fifi-Fifi is incredibly beautiful and I'm sure Geoffrey-Geoffrey is incredibly handsome, so if they did have children they would be so incredibly, incredibly beautiful that mere visibles like us would be struck blind if we looked at them and we would sort of be the proud grandparents.'

Part of Nerlin wanted to tell Dispepsya that she was a complete fruit loop, but another part – the bit with the virus infection – thought that the invisible babies sounded wonderful and was happy to leave Geoffrey-Geoffrey behind.

You might be a king, Dispepsya said to herself, *but you are such a twit.*

Beyond the Old Crones' caves the path

got much narrower. So they wouldn't fall off the mountain, they had been forced to choose the two skinniest donkeys they could find. Naturally, these were also the two oldest donkeys, and so progress was slow.

They climbed up to another small valley where the clouds had decided it was a good place to have a rest. This meant that the group could barely see a thing – apart from lots of cloud, that is. Their only option was to rely on the two donkeys to follow the right path, which was a really rubbish option because neither of the donkeys had ever been there before and, on account of their old age, had really bad eyesight.

'I've never been here before,' said the first donkey. 'Are we going the right way?'

'On the other hand,' said the second donkey, who had a bit of a sense of humour, 'I've never been here before either. So why are you asking me?'

'I wasn't. I was asking the old lady.'

'Listen, donkey, enough of the "old lady", if you don't mind,' said Dispepsya.

'Yeah, OK,' said the first donkey. 'Considering we could well fall to our death at any moment, I don't think calling you old is anything to worry about.'

'Look at it this way,' said Nerlin, 'can't you see more than one path?'

'No,' said both donkeys.

'This would have to be the right one then, wouldn't it?'

'By "no", I meant no I can't see *any* path,' said the first donkey.

'What she said,' said the second donkey.

'I think it might be better if we went on by foot,' said Nerlin.

'Whose foot?' said one of the donkeys.

'Our own,' Nerlin replied.

'Please yourself,' said the donkeys. 'We'll just wait here for you then.'

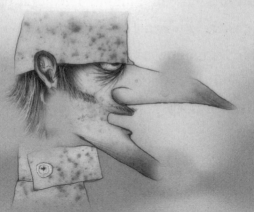

'Halt, who goes there?' said a voice from somewhere in the clouds.

'We do,' said Dispepsya.

'I know that voice,' said Nerlin.

'I know that voice,' said the voice.

'I know those voices,' said a second voice from another part of the cloud.

'What are you two doing here?' said a third voice from a completely different bit of the cloud.

After a lot of banging, crashing, tripping over and cursing, the three Fake Cooks appeared.

'How did you get here ahead of us?' said Dispepsya at exactly the same time the three Fake Cooks said, 'Why did you two come up that way?'

'*We* were wondering about that,' said the two old donkeys.

'We took the shortcut,' said one of the Fake Cooks.

'Shortcut?' said Dispepsya. 'What shortcut?'

After wasting a lot more time, the two donkeys were finally sent back down the shortcut and very soon discovered why it was called a shortcut on account of the fact it was so slippery and steep that they fell off the mountain, which cut their lives short.

The three Fake Cooks, who actually had a printout off Gargle Maps[31] and a proper human GPS,[32] led Nerlin and Dispepsya through the clouds and up another path that eventually took them above the cloud line.

The whole place was like a magical world, which, being part of Transylvania Waters, it was. But it was even more magical. The clouds that they had just climbed through were not the sort of clouds that moved about or leaked water over everyone underneath them. They were Masking Clouds,

---

[31] *Which is like Google Maps PLUS it cures bad breath.*

[32] *Unlike the Transylvania Waters GPS, which stands for Global Pigeon Scout. See* The Floods 10: Lost.

which float above places that are completely secret from the rest of the world. This is why no one has ever seen an aerial photo of Quicklime College, the wizard school in Patagonia. The entire valley is hidden beneath Masking Clouds.

From where they stood, Nerlin and Dispepsya looked out across the tops of the clouds as if they were floating in a big bed of cotton wool. Above them, another Masking Cloud kept them hidden from satellites and cameras floating above the world. This cloud was thick enough to hide them, but thin enough to let the sun's warm glow shine over everything so that it coated the valley with a golden sheen. This was a place that could only be described as perfect.

'We'll leave you now,' said the Fake Cooks. 'We're not really supposed to be up here. Just walk along to the other end of the valley and you'll find Gruinard's house by the Impossible Waterfall.'

'The Impossible Waterfall?' said Nerlin. 'What's that?'

'You'll see.'

Nerlin watched them disappear down the footpath, which seemed to close behind them.

'You could become enchanted by this place,' he said, 'and never want to leave.'

'That's why no one's allowed up here,' Dispepsya explained.

'But we're here.'

'Yes, but Quenelle emailed ahead. We're expected.'

Dispepsya and Nerlin turned and walked along beside the stream, which sparkled and danced like streams do in fairy stories. In fact, it wasn't so much a stream as a babbling brook with brightly coloured kingfishers diving into the water, where beautiful vibrant fish darted among the waving leaves of underwater grasses. It was nature at her most magnificent, apart from the bit at the end when the kingfishers killed the fish and ate them.

'Those poor little fish,' said Dispepsya.

'Sod off, lady,' said one of the kingfishers. 'That's my lunch you're talking about, and yes, they do taste as wonderful as they look.'

They soon discovered that every living thing in the valley could talk, including the fish, though being underwater it was impossible to understand them.

'I wonder what they're saying,' said Dispepsya.

'"Oww" and "ouch", mainly,' said the kingfisher, swooping down for another mouthful.

To their left was a lush meadow full of bright grass and wonderful wildflowers. Here and there, fat happy cows slowly ate their way back to Quenelle's cottage to be milked.

'I feel better already,' said Nerlin. 'Just being here has lifted my spirits. It's as if I've had my head in a paper bag and now it's been taken off.'

They rounded a corner and there was Quenelle's cottage.

The word 'cottage' usually describes somewhere quite small with a thatched roof and roses climbing up the walls, with the whole thing set in a quaint English garden full of delphiniums and dahlias and seventeen other types of flowers all beginning with the letter 'd'.

Quenelle's cottage was exactly like that, except it was very big, was four storeys high and had an attic. True, the roof was thatched, though not with dead reeds but living bushes, long grass and a herd of goats plus a thickening layer of goat poo. True, there were roses climbing up the walls, but their branches were as thick as tree trunks and were home to a tribe of small monkeys. And true, there was a quaint English garden that was doing a magnificent impression of a jungle with a treehouse and a garden pond with two hippopotamuses half-hidden among the waterlilies.

A sweet little old lady appeared from the tangle of flowers and came to greet them.

This can't be Gruinard, thought Nerlin. *Everyone said she was frightening.*

But it was.

'Oh, it's you again,' she snapped at Dispepsya. 'I thought you'd learnt your lesson last time.'

'They made me come,' said Dispepsya.

'Wonderful,' said Gruinard, 'and I am equally delighted to see you. In fact, you can go home now if you like.'

Turning to Nerlin, she changed her tone entirely.

'I am honoured and delighted to meet you, Your Majesty,' she said. 'Though I should really say "meet you again".'

'We've met before?' said Nerlin, slightly anxious that Gruinard might be annoyed because he couldn't remember.

'Many years ago,' said Gruinard. 'You were a small child imprisoned with your family in the drains by your wife's terrible father, who, I am delighted to see in my crystal ball, has just fallen into the raging sea for the seven-hundredth and fifty-third time. What makes it doubly sweet is that it was his terrible wife, the Countess Slab, the woman he deserted your lovely mother-in-law for, who pushed him off their rock seven-hundred and fifty-two times. The other time he slipped.[33]

'Well, I was just a junior witch in those days. I hadn't even taken my first mystic's exam yet,' Gruinard continued. 'My parents were great supporters of your beloved father Merlin and would slip down the mountains at night to creep into the drains and visit your family. I remember singing you to sleep with some of those old Transylvania Waters lullabies.[34] You used to lie in your little sink and

---

[33] *See* The Floods 8: Better Homes and Gardens.

[34] *See the back of the book for examples. Though do remember you will need to obtain a special licence if you actually want to sing any of them yourself.*

gurgle with delight and reach out to Slime Boy with a big grin until you fell fast asleep.'

'Wow,' said Nerlin. 'You can remember more of my childhood than I can.'

'Well, you were only fourteen,' said Gruinard. 'And I must say, it is wonderful to see you again. I wish I had made contact when you came back and reclaimed the throne, but this valley has such a hold on me that I cannot leave it.'

'None of us even knew this place was here,' said Nerlin.

While Dispepsya went back along the path and down through the clouds, which parted to show her the way and closed again when she had passed, Gruinard took Nerlin inside her cottage, sat him down and put the kettle on.

'I think I know what is ailing you,' she called from the kitchen, 'but one can never be certain. First we will have a cup of Gravitea, which will stop you falling over while I do my tests.'

When they had finished their Gravitea and were feeling perfectly balanced, Gruinard took two

sticks of celery and stuck one in each of Nerlin's ears. She put two fingers in the middle of his forehead, closed her eyes and concentrated.

'Mmm, interesting,' she said.

'What?' said Nerlin, who couldn't hear anything because he had two sticks of celery stuck in his ears.

'Well, you're not suffering from celeriac or any other green vegetables,' said Gruinard. 'I'd have sworn you had a touch of broccoli.'

'Oh no,' said Nerlin. 'I've never touched broccoli, not since Geoffrey-Geoffrey told me it could give you global warming.'

'Geoffrey-Geoffrey?' said Gruinard. 'How come I haven't heard of this person?'

Nerlin then spent ten minutes explaining about his invisible friend and how he had come into his life around about the time he began feeling strange, odd, ill, spaced-out and weird, though not necessarily in that order.

'Geoffrey-Geoffrey has been of great comfort to me,' said Nerlin.

88

'Or maybe a curse,' Gruinard suggested.

'No, no, of course not. Geoffrey-Geoffrey is my friend,' said Nerlin.

'Don't you think it's a bit strange that he turned up at exactly the same time you got ill?' said Gruinard.

'Oh no,' said Nerlin.

Let's remember, Nerlin didn't have many close friends, so the idea that Geoffrey-Geoffrey might be less than wonderful was not something he wanted to think about.

'Is he here now?' Gruinard asked.

'Umm, yes.'

'Well, maybe we should make him into a visible friend so I could meet him,' said Gruinard.

Nerlin was horrified. There were so many things to consider. Supposing Geoffrey-Geoffrey was really ugly? If he was short and spotty and fat and looked Belgian, would Nerlin still be able to have him as a special friend? And, of course, if he said that out loud, then it would make Nerlin look really shallow. On the other hand, supposing he was

really, really handsome? Could Nerlin handle that?

I mean, supposing my beloved Mordonna saw him and fell in love with him? Nerlin thought. *What would happen then?*

'I suppose you're wondering how you would feel if Geoffrey-Geoffrey turns out to be really, really ugly?' said Gruinard. 'Or really, really handsome?'

Nerlin shook his head, but his bright-red blushing gave him away.

And of course there was also the nagging thought in the back of his brain: *What if Geoffrey-Geoffrey isn't actually real, but just a figment of my imagination?*

'Though I suspect your biggest fear is finding out that Geoffrey-Geoffrey doesn't really exist and is just part of your imagination,' Gruinard continued. 'If that were the case, it would probably mean you are in a Doolally-overload situation.'

Nerlin looked really embarrassed and scared.

'It's all right,' said Gruinard. 'You wouldn't be human if you didn't have those worries.'

'But I'm not human,' said Nerlin. 'I'm a wizard.'

'Oh yes, of course you are,' said Gruinard. 'Still.'

'What?' said Nerlin.

'Maybe we should just let Geoffrey-Geoffrey stay invisible for now.'

'Yes,' said Nerlin, feeling very relieved.

'In that case, I think the next thing must be the Fruit-Pulp Immersion,' said Gruinard.

She reached up and pulled a calendar down from a shelf and studied it with increasing excitement.

'This is amazing,' she said. 'Tonight is just about the most perfect time in the past one hundred and fifty-three years for a true Fruit-Pulp Immersion. And after tonight it will be at least another three hundred years before such an auspicious night comes again.'

'Wow, that's brilliant,' said Nerlin. 'Why?'

'Well, tonight is Midsummer's Night,' Gruinard explained. 'Today we have an equinox, a solstice, a full moon and buckets and buckets of very ripe fruit. If I were to consult the Fruit-Pulp Oracle – and I'll send her an email right now – I imagine she would be overwhelmed by the incredible coincidensity of it all.'

'Um, what exactly is a Fruit-Pulp Immersion?' said Nerlin.

'Well, it's just amazing,' Gruinard explained. 'Oh look, the Fruit-Pulp Oracle has replied: "Wow, Gruny, I'm overwhelmed by the incredible coincidensity. I will see you at midnight at the Fruit-Pulp Pool". Right, we've got a lot to do.'

She rang a bell and a young girl appeared.

'I want you to collect the others and fill the Fruit-Pulp Pool to the very brim with the finest fruit pulp you can get. Spare no expense, for tonight's ceremony will go down in history as the greatest Fruit-Pulp Immersion in the entire history of Fruit-Pulp Immersions. Also, I need you to send word down to Quenelle and the other Old Crones and tell them all – and I mean every one of them – to be here at eleven-thirty. They must each have a bath, even if it has been less than a year since their last, and they are to wear their finest sacks, for tonight they too may bathe in the greatest Fruit-Pulp Immersion the world has ever seen. And be sure to tell them to bring a towel.'

'And shall we sieve the fruit pulp through the enchanted cobweb, mistress?' said the girl.

'Absolutely not,' said Gruinard. 'Tonight the Fruit-Pulp Immersion will be the full bio-dynamic recipe – natural as nature intended, pips and all.'

Now, Nerlin had always been a fairly down-to-earth sort of person, or as down-to-earth as a wizard can be. So the idea of jumping into a pond of fruit salad seemed a little bit weird and hippy-like.[35] Would he have to take all his clothes off in front of everyone, or were there special Fruit-Pulp Immersion swimmers that you could wear? And were you supposed to drink some of the pulp after everyone had been swimming in it with their dirty feet and pimples and hair? Did you have to put your head right under? And if you did, what would

---

[35] *Many years ago in the 1960s, I lived in a beautiful village in Deiá, Mallorca, where one of the world's most famous poets, Robert Graves, lived. Robert kept getting letters from strange hippy groups in California after one of his books became a sort of hippy bible. One letter invited Robert to come to a commune on Midsummer's Night so that he could join a Fruit-Pulp Immersion.*

happen if you got raspberries stuck up your nose? It all seemed a bit dangerous and ridiculous.

On the other hand, the sensible bit of his brain told himself, *it probably isn't a real Fruit-Pulp Immersion. It's more likely to be a sort of symbolic thing where you just stick your finger in a jar of strawberry jam.*

And we've all done that, haven't we?

Nerlin certainly had, though he preferred a pot of honey.

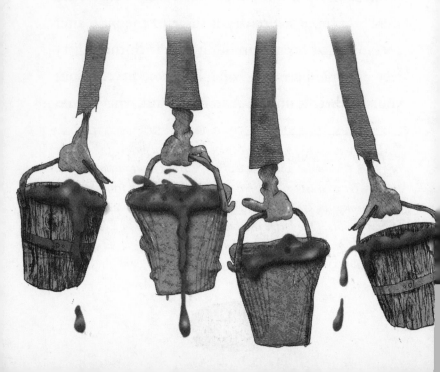

But no, it wasn't going to be a jam jar. The sound of singing approached and, looking out of the window, Nerlin saw fifteen trainee witches carrying huge buckets of squashed fruit along the path and up into the trees beyond the Impossible Waterfall.

Two minutes later, fifteen trainee wizards went by, also carrying buckets of mushy fruit, and two minutes after that, another fifteen witches, and so it went on until sunset.

'Tell me something,' Nerlin asked, trying to get Fruit-Pulp Immersion thoughts out of his head, 'why is it called the Impossible Waterfall?'

'I'll show you,' said Gruinard. 'Follow me.'

They left the cottage and walked up to where the waterfall came crashing down into the stream. The water was clearer than glass and shinier than the shiniest glass that ever came out of a dishwasher. It was only a narrow strip of water, no more than a metre wide, but it fell from a fantastic height.

Looking up, Nerlin could see it falling out of a layer of Masking Clouds.

'Yes, it's beautiful,' he said, 'but why is it called impossible?'

Gruinard raised her arms in the air and concentrated. Slowly, the clouds parted to reveal the source of the waterfall.

There wasn't one.

'See?' she said.

'I can't see anything,' said Nerlin.

'Exactly.'

'But . . .'

There was nothing there. The waterfall just appeared out of thin air and fell down into the stream.

Gruinard lowered her arms and the Masking Clouds slid back into place.

'That's impossible,' said Nerlin.

'Exactly,' said Gruinard.

The waterfall, although impossible, was beautiful in its simplicity. Gruinard said it had been there for as long as anyone could remember and it was the reason she had built her house where it was. The water itself, she said, was the one true fountain

of youth, though you had to be very careful where you drank it from.

'If you take a glass from the stream after it has passed my garden gate, it actually makes you get older,' she explained, 'and the further downstream you go, the quicker you age. To get the maximum effect you must hold the glass in the flow of water as it comes down from the sky.'

'Wow,' said Nerlin. 'Think I could do with a glass of that.'

'You will tomorrow, after tonight's Fruit-Pulp Immersion,' said Gruinard. 'There are some people who believe that if you went up the waterfall to where the water appears and drank some of that, you would actually get younger and younger until you were a child again.'

At eleven o'clock, the Old Crones arrived and everyone walked up the path behind the waterfall. They climbed a short flight of stone steps and there, set in a tiny flat lawn of brilliant grass, was the Fruit-Pulp Pool. It was so close to the back of the waterfall that a fine mist of spray filled the air.

The moon was full, just edging towards the highest point in the sky. The Old Crones, bathed in its eerie blue light, held out their hands, let the mist settle on their faces and slowly massaged the water into their skin. The effects were instant and amazing. The Old Crones became the Young Crones as their wrinkles disappeared.

'Why have you never come up here before?'

asked Nerlin, who could feel the lines on his own face smoothing over as the mist condensed on his skin. He wondered if he could take a couple of bottles back for Mordonna, but he suspected, correctly, that the magic would not work once the water left the valley.

'It is forbidden,' said Quenelle. 'The entrance to this valley closes over and only opens at Gruinard's command.'

'And why is she not young and beautiful?' Nerlin whispered to Quenelle.

'The waterfall creates magic, not miracles,' Quenelle replied. 'She is over seven hundred years old. So, really, she's pretty good for her age.'

As midnight approached, Gruinard came up the path and stood in front of everyone.

'Right, everybody,' she said. 'Clothes off and into the Fruit-Pulp Immersion.'

'What?' said Nerlin, fearing the worst.

'I said, clothes off . . .'

'I heard what you said,' said Nerlin, 'but it's embarrassing. I mean, I'm the only man here.'

'It's all right,' said Quenelle, throwing her sackcloth onto the pile with everyone else's. 'Just keep your eyes shut.'

'But everyone will see my body,' Nerlin protested.

'Yes, but if you shut your eyes, you won't be able to see them looking at you,' Quenelle explained.

'What? No, that's not right! Everyone else should keep their eyes shut, not me,' said Nerlin.

'But then you'd be able to see all of our bodies,' said one of the Young Crones. 'And we are all young and lovely now.'

'I can see you all now,' said Nerlin, who was the only one left with clothes on.

So the Young Crones all slipped discreetly into the fruit pulp and immersed themselves up to their necks.

'Is that better?' said Quenelle.

'Yes, but you can still see me,' said Nerlin.

'Well, we'll look up at the moon and hum a little song,' said Gruinard.

So Nerlin stripped off and lowered himself into the Fruit-Pulp Immersion. And apart from one Young Crone who just couldn't help herself, no one saw Nerlin being nude. The one who did giggled, and thought, *Ooer, I don't know what he's wearing, but it needs ironing,* and wished she had been looking at the moon too.

Far, far away, deep down in the valley, the solstice bell in the tower of Castle Twilight, which only rang twice a year, chimed midnight. As its echo died, the Old Crones began chanting and formed a ring around Nerlin.

One by one they tapped him on the head until the last one, Quenelle, left her hand there and suddenly, with no warning, pushed Nerlin Flood, the King of Transylvania Waters, under the surface of the Fruit-Pulp Pool, holding him there while he spluttered and struggled. Just as Nerlin thought he was going to drown, she took her hand away and he came up and took a huge breath of air.

'Ahh, oooh, oooooooooooooooh, errr,' he cried, wiping the fruit from his eyes.

'You might have warned me you were going to do that . . .'

There was no one there.

Except there was, and Nerlin could feel it wriggling around in the bottom of the Fruit-Pulp Pool. It slid over his feet and tried to bite him.

Forgetting he was naked, Nerlin leapt out of the pool. The fruit pulp covered him from head to toe like a thick skin. It stuck to him like a suit of clothes.

'How are you feeling?' Gruinard asked, coming back up the path.

'There's something swimming around in the bottom of the pool,' Nerlin said.

'No there isn't.'

'There is,' Nerlin insisted. 'It wriggled across my feet.'

'Well, it isn't one of the crones,' said Gruinard. 'They're all back at my house now, getting showered and dressed.'

'No, it was much smaller than a person.'

'Maybe a rat fell in the pool.'

'No, it was bigger than a rat.'

And as they watched, the level of the Fruit-Pulp Pool began to drop. It got lower and lower, until a writhing creature the size of a dog appeared. It was very fat and was drinking the fruit pulp, a feat that seemed impossible, seeing as the pulp volume was a thousand times bigger than the creature's size.

Gruinard threw a bucket of water over the creature. And it was then that they could see that it was nothing at all like a dog.

It was a short, hideous homunculus.[36] Above

---

[36] *Look it up on Google, and despite what you might think the female version is NOT a homauntulus. Actually, I have decided that it is.*

a minute, hairless body with skinny arms and legs and enormous hands and feet was the ugliest head Gruinard and Nerlin had ever seen.

'Toiletbrain!' it cursed. 'Toe-cheese-pigface!'

'Oh my God!' cried Nerlin, and fainted.

The voice was a voice he had heard inside his head many, many times.

It was Geoffrey-Geoffrey.

Gruinard may have been very old, but her brain was faster than the speed of light. In a split second she slid shut the steel grating for when the Fruit-Pulp Pool wasn't being used so that Geoffrey-Geoffrey was imprisoned there. There were seventeen bolts around the rim of the pool and Gruinard ran around frantically, slamming each one shut.

Then she threw several buckets of water from the Impossible Waterfall over Nerlin, dried him off and got him back into his clothes.

'I just had a terrible nightmare,' he said when he came around. 'There was this gross creature in the pool, like an evil little homunculus, and it had killed Geoffrey-Geoffrey and stolen his voice.'

'It wasn't a nightmare,' said Gruinard as she and the Young Crones, who were now the Middle-Aged Crones[37] as the waterfall spell wore off, pushed a lot of big heavy rocks onto the steel grating, just to make sure Geoffrey-Geoffrey stayed put.

'Lemmeout, lemmeout, lemmeout!' he screamed.

Nerlin peered over the edge of the pit at the creature, who was now bright red with anger.

'What have you done with Geoffrey-Geoffrey?' Nerlin shouted.

'I *am* Geoffrey-Geoffrey, you horrible old man,' he sneered at him.

'Don't be stupid,' said Nerlin. 'Geoffrey-Geoffrey is my friend. He is kind and helpful and wonderful.'

'You are a very stupid old man,' Geoffrey-

---

[37] *Oh, come on! Surely you didn't think the amazing wonderful effect of the Impossible Waterfall would last forever? You'll be eating Royal Jelly and drinking Immortalitea next. By the way, have you ever noticed how all the people selling things that make you live forever always look quite old, unhealthy and tatty?*

Geoffrey said, and laughed. 'I was never your friend. I just pretended to be, after what you all did to my mother!'

'What are you talking about?' said Nerlin. 'I've never even met your mother.'

'Your family destroyed her. First, you imprisoned her at the bottom of the sea and then you totally destroyed her. And all she was doing was her job as a good and devoted servant to your wretched wife's father,' said Geoffrey-Geoffrey.

'You mean, your mother was the vile and evil Hearse Whisperer?' said Gruinard.

'No, my mother was the kind and lovely Hearse Whisperer,' Geoffrey-Geoffrey whimpered. 'A finer mother no boy could ask for.

'Even if she did desert us all when were little children,' he added.

'And turn us into homunculi,' he continued, 'and eat our father.

'And leave us all alone in an orphanage on the edge of Ulan Bator,' he concluded.

'If all that's a description of a kind and lovely

mother,' Gruinard said, 'what on earth is a bad mother like?'

'Well, she never made us watch *Australia's Got Talent* or eat greasy takeaway burgers,' said Geoffrey-

Geoffrey. 'Though, come to think of it, neither of them existed when we were babies.'

'So you have brothers and sisters?' said Nerlin.

'I did,' said Geoffrey-Geoffrey. 'I had seven sisters, but they came to a sticky end.'

'So you are all alone in the world?' said Gruinard.

'No, I'm all alone in this disgusting sticky pit,' Geoffrey-Geoffrey sneered. 'And if you don't let me out this instant you'll regret it.'

'Really?' said Gruinard. 'You have wizard powers then?'

'No.'

'So how will I, second only in witch power to Mordonna, Queen of Transylvania Waters, regret it?'

Geoffrey-Geoffrey didn't answer. He splashed around knee-deep in the dregs of the Fruit-Pulp Immersion, cursing, swearing and saying every rude word he could think of, as well as some new and promising ones he made up as he went along.

'I think we will just leave you down there for

now,' said Gruinard, 'until you calm down a bit. Someone will bring you some food later.'

'I don't want your stinking dinner,' said Geoffrey-Geoffrey. 'I'll just eat the rest of this fruit pulp.'

'Please yourself,' said Gruinard, and she and Nerlin went back down to the cottage.

When they had had a few hours' sleep and a very bacony breakfast, the Ageless Crones sat Nerlin down and questioned him.

'So do you feel any different after the Fruit-Pulp Immersion?' was the question everyone asked.

'Dn't thnk s,' said Nerlin. 'Spps m bt clmr.'

'What?' said Quenelle, wriggling her fingers in her ears. 'Can you repeat that? I didn't quite catch it.'

'Sd, spps fl bt clmr,' said Nerlin.

'I think he's lost control of his vowels,' said Gruinard. 'Repeat after me: a b d c d e f g h i o u.'

'Wht n rth fr?'

'Just do it, please,' Gruinard repeated. 'A b d c d e f g h i o u.'

'B d c d f g h,' said Nerlin.

'Yes, just as I thought. Our beloved King has lost control of his vowels,' said Gruinard.

'What are we going to do?' said Quenelle. 'I imagine there's a cure of some sort?'

'Yes, there is,' said Gruinard.

She left the room and came back with a great big baggy pair of underpants, which she handed to Nerlin.

'You'll need to wear these, Your Majesty,' she said. 'Go into the downstairs bathroom and put them on under your other clothes. Oh, and don't forget to tuck them into your socks.'

'Wht r thy?' said Nerlin.

'They are Incompetence Pants,' Gruinard explained. 'You'll need to wear them for a few days until your vowels are working properly again. It's nothing to worry about, it's just a very rare side-effect of the Fruit-Pulp Immersion and it will eventually wear off.'

It was agreed that Nerlin would stay at Gruinard's cottage until all was back to normal. No one wanted his family or his subjects to see him

talking without his vowels. They would all think he
was certainly Doolally.

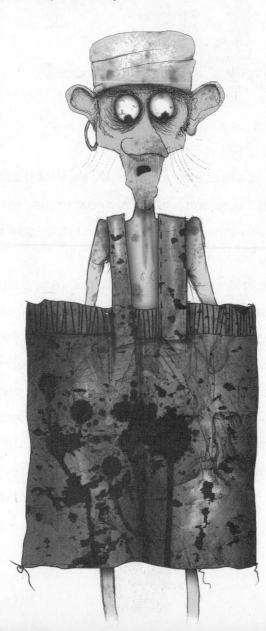

IT'S A NINE
THAT'S
FALLEN
OVER A BIT.

CUCKOO

Meanwhile, after a night so cold that the last of the Fruit-Pulp Immersion left in the pool froze over, turning his legs blue, Geoffrey-Geoffrey was in no mood to 'calm down'.

He had been angry when the fruit pulp had been warmed by the bodies of the chanting crones. He stamped his feet, breaking the layer of ice and desperately trying to think of some new swear words that would be worse than all the ones he had used the day before. Then the sun rose over the high mountains, and the whole valley was filled with its beautiful golden light, but instead of making Geoffrey-Geoffrey feel a bit warmer and a bit happier, it shone right into his eyes and blinded him.

It was one of those days.

And if anyone knew about those sorts of days, it was Geoffrey-Geoffrey.

Since he had been abandoned by his mother in the world's most remote orphanage with no chance of ever being rescued, he had lived a cursed life.

Food in the orphanage had consisted of snow, pine needles and boiled newspapers. One by one, his seven sisters had fallen prey to cannibals, he himself having eaten at least two burgers before discovering who they were. He had only survived by collecting all the diseases he could find. A fine collection of bubonic plague, massive leaking boils, pimples, verrucas, blackheads and abscesses had meant even the hungriest savage had refused to eat him.

By the time he had been old enough to leave the orphanage, he had grown fond of his revolting disfigurements, so that when nature stepped in and showed him a kindness he did not deserve by curing most of his diseases, he managed to hang onto a few particularly colourful boils by continually digging at them with a rusty fork.

Once free of the orphanage, Geoffrey-Geoffrey walked out of Mongolia during the coldest winter anyone could remember. It had been so cold that all the thermometers had frozen solid, and so no one could actually tell just how cold it had been.

To this day there are seven of Geoffrey-Geoffrey's toes and three fingers frozen solid in remote snowdrifts. On the warmest day of the year, when the ice melts down to a mere seven metres thick, Geoffrey-Geoffrey can hear his missing digits calling out to him from their frozen tombs.[38]

By the time he'd reached civilisation and places where the ground wasn't just grey and white, Geoffrey-Geoffrey was frozen through to the marrow in his bones and he has stayed that way ever since, even if he visits places where the sun shines all day and there are heatwaves.

When he saw fresh green grass for the first

---

[38] *They are not alone. It has been estimated that there are over seventeen thousand toes, fingers, ears and noses frozen into the arctic tundra of outer Mongolia. There are other lost bits of bodies out there too, but we won't go there.*

time, he was so overwhelmed that he couldn't move. He stood on the front lawn of a suburban garden in a small Russian town and just stared at the trees and flowers, completely hypnotised.

'Oh, look, Sergei,' said the lady of the house, 'someone has left a garden gnome on our front lawn.'

'Quick,' said Sergei, 'let us carry it into the back garden before anyone sees and thinks we have come into a fortune.'

So Geoffrey-Geoffrey stood in the back garden, still unable to move, and for the next three weeks he stared at Sergei and Irenka's outside lavatory, though calling six planks put together with second-hand nails, a leaky cardboard bucket, and a half-eaten horse blanket a lavatory was a bit of an overstatement.

But someone had seen Sergei carrying Geoffrey-Geoffrey into their back garden, and one dark night the thief threw him into a sack and carried him off. This brought Geoffrey-Geoffrey out of his trance, and three days later all that was found of the thief were his broken false teeth, his left kneecap and a small part of the sack.

Full of roasted thief, Geoffrey-Geoffrey then crossed Russia and reached Ukraine, still unsure of where he was aiming for.

He only had one link to his past. He might have had more when he was dumped as a baby in the orphanage, but anything of the tiniest value had been taken from him within five minutes of his arrival. However, there was one clue that could not be so easily stolen. In his left armpit was the following tattoo:

```
St. Ghoul's Hospital
Transylvania Waters
Baby number: 667
```

Like most people, he had never heard of Transylvania Waters and his total lack of any education meant that he couldn't read or write, so that even if he had heard of Transylvania Waters, he wouldn't have known it was written in his armpit. In fact, he had hardly learnt to speak, and the tiny vocabulary he did have was from a very obscure version of the Mongolian language.

116

But every cloud has a silver lining, even for a creature as vile as Geoffrey-Geoffrey, and not long after escaping from the gnome thief, he was discovered whimpering in a ditch by a kindly, old turnip-farmer's wife, Berylinka, whose one regret in life had been that she had never had any children or puppies.

In Geoffrey-Geoffrey she realised she had both, and had showered him with love and nice things.[39] The only thing she did wrong was dress him in girl's clothes. This was not because she didn't realise he was a boy, but because she had a whole drawer full of girl's clothes, waiting for the daughter she had never had. Luckily, Geoffrey-Geoffrey actually liked wearing dresses.

Now, Berylinka was not a simple peasant but a university graduate who had become a simple peasant's wife when her father had lost her in a card game. And so it was that she gave Geoffrey-Geoffrey

---

[39] *Nice by Ukranian standards of the day: his own made-to-measure cardboard boots, a red rubber ball with almost no teeth marks and a toy pistol carved out of a mammoth's shinbone.*

117

an education. In no time at all he became fluent in trigonometry and advanced microbiology, but he still couldn't read or write. But by another wonderful twist of fate, it turned out that Berylinka's husband was not actually a simple peasant either, but a secret agent posing as one.

'This is news to me, Joseph,' Berylinka said to her husband.

'That, my darlingski, is because I am a secret agent,' Joseph explained. 'In fact, I am so secret that for the first fifteen years, even I did not know I was a secret agent.'

Joseph was also a university graduate, with seven degrees in foreign languages. And so it was that Geoffrey-Geoffrey learned to read and write and finally discovered what his tattoo said.

'That is a stroke of good luck, my little babushky,' said Berylinka. 'If you travel to our easternmost border you will cross into Transylvania Waters, or so I have been told.'

'Then, Muminski,' Geoffrey-Geoffrey said, 'that is where I must go.'

'But you will come back to us, won't you?' said Berylinka and Joseph. 'For we love you like a daughter, sorry, like a son.'

'I will,' said Geoffrey-Geoffrey. 'For you have shown me more kindness than anyone. But I must go back to my roots if only to exact terrible revenge on a mother who so cruelly abandoned me.'

'Indeed, that is our way,' said Berylinka.

'In the meantime,' said Joseph, 'now that Berylinka and I know each other as clever university

graduates and not the simple peasants we pretended to be, we shall pass our days playing Scrabble and doing Mensa tests.'

'Too right,' said Berylinka. 'Stuff the turnips.'

A week later, wearing his best frock, Geoffrey-Geoffrey was knocking on the door of St Ghoul's Hospital. The office staff, having spent a long time admiring his lovely dress, found the records for baby 667 and Geoffrey-Geoffrey discovered who his mother was. He also discovered that Nerlin, the King of Transylvania Waters, and the rest of the Floods had destroyed her.

He vowed total revenge, total in that it would mean the complete annihilation of the entire Floods family.

'I will start at the top with the King and work down to the tiniest grandchild,' he said. 'I will not rest until I have destroyed them all.'

No one had told him that the Floods were a family of wizards, but he was so wound up it wouldn't have stopped him anyway.

'First, I shall find an evil witch and buy an Invisibility Spell,' he said to himself. 'And then I shall ask: Why have I no knowledge of my father? Followed by: Do I have any other living relatives?'

As Geoffrey-Geoffrey marched backwards and forwards in the bottom of the Fruit-Pulp Pool, cursing and thinking that things couldn't get any worse, he caught his foot on something and fell flat on his face. He opened his mouth to swear and got a mouthful of fruit pulp that had begun to ferment, but at least it distracted him briefly from the prune that found its way up his left nostril and the drowned sparrow up his right.

He stood up, spat out the pulp and pulled the stuff out of his nose, though a tail feather had become

deeply embedded in his sinuses and would forever vibrate in an infuriatingly tickly way every time he sneezed. He bent down and felt through the pulp until he found what it was that had tripped him.

It was a large iron ring.

'The sort of ring you get on a sink plug,' he said to himself, and pulled it.

It was jammed tight, but he kept pulling until at last the plug came free.

As the pulp gradually slid down the plughole Geoffrey-Geoffrey sat down to take a rest while the mist from the Impossible Waterfall washed him and the pool clean.

'That plughole,' he said to himself, 'is big enough for me to escape down.'

But you don't know where the drain goes to, a warning voice said inside his head.

'I haven't got to where I am today by listening to warning voices,' he said.

Yes, but look where you are *today,* the voice said.

'Shut up.'

Geoffrey-Geoffrey had learned a long time

ago that even when he did listen to warning voices, it didn't seem to make much difference. Ninety-nine times out of a hundred the results had been horrible. The only good thing he could remember, the one time in a hundred, had been when Berylinka had found him in the ditch. And on that occasion no warning voices had been involved anyway. So, in reality, listening to warning voices had ended up being useless one hundred times out of one hundred, which was exactly the same odds as ignoring them.

So Geoffrey-Geoffrey eased himself into the drain. At the last minute he thought he might like to change his mind, but it was too late. The sides of the drain were completely smooth and lubricated with slimy fruit pulp so there was no way of stopping.

'Gone down the plughole, has he?' said Gruinard when she and Quenelle went back up to the pool a bit later.

'Yes, just like you said he would,' Quenelle said.

'And did you implant the tracking device inside him?'

'I did. It's hidden inside a fake cherry stone lodged securely in his appendix,' said Quenelle.

'So at last we shall find out where the drain leads to,' said Gruinard.

'Indeed,' said Quenelle. 'And I would imagine it must be somewhere very important, considering it carries the sacred Fruit-Pulp dregs.'

Back in Gruinard's cottage, the two Old Crones, who, now the Fruit-Pulp Immersion had worn off, were old again, opened the secret door under the stairs and went down into the secret room, where Gruinard kept all her gadgets and inventions, most of which had been inspired by a well-thumbed copy of *Professor Winchflat's Wonder Book of Inventions*.

When the two Old Crones checked the tracking machine they saw the tiny device buried in Geoffrey-Geoffrey's stomach leap and jump and wriggle across the screen. Sometimes it would stop, as if looking around, and then move on.

124

'If only the device had audio so we could hear what he is saying,' said Quenelle.

'It does,' said Gruinard. 'I just forgot to turn it on.'

'M gttng brd,' said Nerlin. 'Nd mss my wf.'

'Ah, you got your "y" back,' said Quenelle. 'They always come back first because they're not a proper vowel, but it does mean that it shouldn't be too long now before the proper vowels start returning. I think we'll go back down to my cave this afternoon.'

It was then that Nerlin realised how much he had fallen under the enchanting spell of Gruinard's hidden valley and the Impossible Waterfall. A large part of him wanted to stay there forever, and if he could have clicked his fingers to bring his family up there to be with him, he would have done so in an instant.

'But you are the King,' said Gruinard. 'You have

a responsibility to this country and your people. You can't just abandon them and live up here.'

'Cn cme here when retre?' said Nerlin.

'Ah, got your "e" back now, Your Majesty,' said Gruinard. 'But will you really retire? That's not how kings and queens work. They stay on their thrones long past the age they should. They do that, because, let's be honest, they don't really have any power, nor do they do anything useful, so they carry on long after their brains stop working.'

'I dn't wnt t d tht,' said Nerlin, who now only had his "o"s and "a"s to recover. 'I wnt t build little cttge up here nd grw flwers nd brussels spruts.'

'But it's the tradition,' said Quenelle. 'You can't go against tradition, especially as you're a king. If kings and queens can't keep out-of-date, silly things alive, who can?'

'Then we will change tradition,' Nerlin insisted with all his vowels functioning smoothly again. 'Transylvania Waters will lead the world. I shall retire, and my eldest child will become King while he and I still have some working brain cells left.'

'I suppose it could work,' Gruinard agreed. 'Though it's never been done before.'

'But if I do it,' said Nerlin, 'you wouldn't mind if I build a little cottage for Mordonna and me up here?'

'I welcome you to, Your Majesty.'

'Wonderful,' said Nerlin. 'By the way, can I take my Incompetence Pants off now?'

'You don't want to keep them as a souvenir?'

Nerlin thought probably not, especially since they had some embarrassing raspberry stains. He then asked about Geoffrey-Geoffrey and was worried to hear he had escaped down a drain.

'And where do the drains lead to?' he asked.

'We're tracking him at the moment,' said Gruinard, 'with our cherry-pip cam.'

'Yes,' said Quenelle, 'and we're placing bets on where he'll end up. Do you want to wager a few dolors?'[40]

---

[40] *In case you haven't seen* The Amazing Illustrated Floodsopedia, *the money in Transylvania Waters is Scents and Dolors.*

Nerlin decided he would have a small bet, if only to take his mind off things. These were the choices:

- *In Lake Tarnish – most likely outcome. ODDS of 3 to 2.*
- *In the drains beneath Dreary – fairly likely. ODDS of 1 to 1.*[41]
- *In the main kitchen sink of Castle Twilight. ODDS of 3 to 1.*
- *Back in the Fruit-Pulp Pool because the drains are a möbius strip. ODDS of 9 to 1.*
- *Somewhere in Belgium – we can only hope. ODDS of 25 to 1.*
- *A small hole in Rockall – incredibly unlikely. ODDS of 3000^{17} to 1.*[42]

---

[41] *Actually, pretty unlikely because since Nerlin became King, the drains of his childhood have become a top tourist attraction with more than fourteen visitors a year.*

[42] PLEASE NOTE: *The 17 on this line does NOT refer to a footnote – it is a mathematical number meaning 3000 to the power of seventeen.*

Nerlin – knowing that Mordonna's father and the awful Countess Slab were banished to Rockall and he had organised for the Hearse Whisperer, who had been stored in a deep freeze, to be broken into hailstone-sized bits and dropped on Rockall – decided to place twelve dolors on Rockall.[43]

[43] See Floods 8: Better Homes & Gardens *to find out why Rockall is important and how the Hearse Whisperer had ended up frozen.*

'Are you sure?' said Gruinard. 'We only put that option in as a joke.'

'I have a bad feeling about that,' said Nerlin and told them why.

'We'd better go down to the cellar and see where Geoffrey-Geoffrey's got to then,' said Gruinard.

The room was almost in total darkness, lit only by the tracking screen, which glowed green on the main table. Gruinard sat down and beckoned Nerlin to sit beside her. A small red dot moved slowly and jerkily across the screen, stopping briefly, then shooting forward a bit before settling down to a steady drift towards the top left corner of the display.

'Why is it moving so erratically?' said Nerlin.

'I suppose it must speed up when it comes to a steep drop and the little pause each time is probably Geoffrey-Geoffrey trying to hold on to something to slow himself down,' said Gruinard.

The red dot stopped moving. Nerlin and Gruinard stared at it in silence for a few minutes, but it stayed exactly where it was.

'Damn,' said Gruinard.

'What's happened?' said Nerlin.

'Well, Geoffrey-Geoffrey is possibly asleep, but it's unlikely. I mean, would you want to sleep in a dirty old drain, Your Majesty?'

'I did every night for the first twenty years of my life,' said Nerlin.

'Oh, I forgot. I'm so sorry,' said Gruinard. 'Of course, he could be stuck, or dead, or just having a bit of a rest.'

'There is another option,' said Nerlin.

'Which is?'

'Well, he could have pooed out the cherry stone and be miles away by now.'

'I don't think so,' said Gruinard. 'We put little tiny hooks in the stone so it would anchor itself into his gut and stay there.'

She picked up an intercom and spoke.

'Can you hear me up there?'

'Yes,' said a voice.

'Put the chain back on the plug and place it into the plug hole,' Gruinard instructed. 'Then put the big funnel under the Impossible Waterfall and

guide the outlet into the Fruit-Pulp Pool and fill it up. When the water reaches the top, pull the chain and let the water go. I want to give the drain a great big flush-out.'

Gruinard pressed a switch and an image appeared on the screen. It was a map overlay that showed where in the world Geoffrey-Geoffrey was.

'Right in the middle of Belgium,' said Gruinard and, pressing a button, added, 'let's see if we can hear anything.'

There was a faint blurry noise.

'I would say that's snoring,' said Nerlin. Gruinard agreed.

As they watched there was a loud muffled sound and the red dot shot forward on the screen with lots of angry noises that could only have been swear words.

It was obvious that the water had arrived, flushing Geoffrey-Geoffrey out of his resting place. Within two minutes of it appearing he had crossed the English Channel and was racing north towards Scotland, and it was here that he began to slow down.

It took two more good Fruit-Pulp Pool flushes to get Geoffrey-Geoffrey back up to speed and finally he left the Scottish coast and headed out to sea.

Rockall is such a tiny rock that it was impossible to see it on the map, but a couple of minutes later that was where Geoffrey-Geoffrey came to a sudden and final halt.

He had arrived.

'What is twelve dolors times three thousand to the power of seventeen?' said Nerlin.

'Well, off the top of my head,' said Quenelle, 'it's approximately 286,511,799,958,070, which I think is more than all the money in the whole world added together.'

'Hey, now that means you own the entire world and everything,' said Gruinard. 'Don't spend it all at once!'

'Right,' said Nerlin.

It was still hailing little frozen bits of his mother when Geoffrey-Geoffrey came flying out of a crack in the rocks. He shot out with such force, followed by a huge gush of water, that it sent Ex-King Quatorze – who had been crouching right in front of it trying to hide from his beloved wife, the revolting, rude, overweight, lumpy, spotty, smelling-of-dead-fish and generally bad-tempered Countess Slab – crashing right into the aforementioned Slab's very big bottom.

'Don't think you can get back in my good books by flirting with me,' she cried, as she went headfirst into the sea for the seventh time that day.

'I wasn't, my beloved,' Ex-King Quatorze said,

helping her out of the violent waves. 'Something hit me in the back.'

'Something? Something?' Countess Slab snapped. 'There ain't no something here. There's only you, me and these dirty frozen hailstones.'

'And there's the something,' said the ex-King. 'Look.' He pointed to where Geoffrey-Geoffrey had fallen down a hole between two rocks and was whimpering in a state of semi-consciousness.

'Oh my God, what is that?' said the Countess, poking Geoffrey-Geoffrey with a stick.[44]

He may have been semi-conscious, but Geoffrey-Geoffrey's reflexes were as sharp as his temper. He grabbed the end of the Countess's stick and gave it a violent tug, which took her by such surprise that she let go of it.

---

[44] *The Countess's stick deserves a mention here. Rockall is, as its name suggests, all rock. There are no trees, no grass, no anything. Except rock. The only green things are bits of seaweed the ocean has vomited up onto the rock and the colour of Ex-King Quatorze's skin most of the time. Other things get thrown up on Rockall every now and then, and Countess Slab's stick was one of them.*

'Right, lumpy,' he said, jumping out of the hole. 'Where the hell am I and when is the next train out of here?'

'Rockall,' said Ex-King Quatorze.

'Don't you swear at me,' Geoffrey-Geoffrey shouted.

'No, stupid,' said the ex-King. 'That's where you are – Rockall.'

He led Geoffrey-Geoffrey up to the highest point of the forsaken rock and waved his arm around.

'See? Rockall,' he said. 'No train, no more land, no escape, just miles and miles of very angry cold waves for as far as the eye can see in every direction.'

'And believe me, we've tried to leave,' said the Countess. 'Every single bloomin' day for what feels like a hundred years, we've tried.'

'Can't you attract the attention of a passing ship?' said Geoffrey-Geoffrey.

'One: there are no passing ships, and two: there's no way of attracting them if there were,' said the ex-King. 'The only way to do so would be to start a fire, but everything here is constantly drenched by the endless waves.'

'And now there's all this wretched hail,' said the Countess.

As Geoffrey-Geoffrey looked up, a hailstone landed right in his mouth. Before he could spit it out, it melted and Geoffrey-Geoffrey felt himself go faint in the head. He sat down with a thud, reached out and caught a couple more hailstones and popped them in his mouth.

'There is something freakish about this hail,' he said. 'It's like a weird sort of ghost.'

Countess Slab tasted the hail, but she had no feedback to offer. However, when Ex-King Quatorze tasted it, he went from a sickly green colour to a deathly shade of white, a white so bright that for a split second he looked like a tiny lighthouse on top of the rock.

'The Hearse Whisperer,' he said.

'WHAT?' said Geoffrey-Geoffrey.

'The Hearse Whisperer,' Ex-King Quatorze said. 'This hail storm is the Hearse Whisperer.'

'Oh my God,' said Geoffrey-Geoffrey. 'That's my mother.'

'The Hearse Whisperer is your mother?' said the ex-King.

Geoffrey-Geoffrey nodded. He didn't know what to think or say. Nothing in his life up to that point had given him any training on how to react if you found you mother falling around you as tiny hailstones.

'Oh, how touching,' Countess Slab sneered. 'A family reunion.'

There were no buckets or bowls or mugs or jugs or basins or barrels or even plastic bags on Rockall. There was nothing at all to collect the Hearse

Whisperer with as she fell around them, except a few empty scallop shells. The hail increased until it was falling as thick as a snowstorm and then suddenly stopped.

Geoffrey-Geoffrey ran around pushing the piles of hailstones into all the dents in the rock. And then, as they melted, an amazing thing happened. The pools of melted Hearse Whisperer slid out of the smaller pools into bigger pools, where they merged together and when these pools were full, they slid into bigger pools and merged some more. They kept on doing this until they were all together in one large pool, the only large pool on Rockall.

Gradually the liquid grew opaque and rose up out of the pool, until there in front of them was the Hearse Whisperer.

Or rather, quite a lot of her.

The hailstones that had missed Rockall and fallen into the sea were clearly gone, as were the few that Ex-King Quatorze and Geoffrey-Geoffrey had swallowed. So although there was enough of her to exist, she only had one ear and three fingers.

And most of her teeth were missing. As well as her left knee.

'Where am I?' she said. 'And when is the next train out of here?'

'Mother,' said Geoffrey-Geoffrey.

'Mother? Mother?!' said the Hearse Whisperer. 'What are you talking about, you horrible little homunculus?'

'It is I, your firstborn son, Geoffrey-Geoffrey.'

'I have no children,' said the Hearse Whisperer. 'I demand a DNA test. Hold up your hand.'

Geoffrey-Geoffrey did as he was told and instantly regretted it. The Hearse Whisperer bit his little finger off.

'Blimey,' she said as Geoffrey-Geoffrey fainted. 'He is my son.'

The Hearse Whisperer had as much maternal instinct as a bag of cement. Even a bottle of milk that's gone off has more feeling for the bacteria growing in its curdled remains than she did for her long-lost child. Usually when a child and its parent are reunited after many, many years, past hurts and

141

hardships are forgotten. Blood is thicker than water and all that sort of thing, and the deep bonds of family generally overlook, or at least forgive, all the bad memories.

The Hearse Whisperer was not like this. Neither was Geoffrey-Geoffrey.

Yes, he is my long-lost son, she thought, *and I wish he still was long-lost.*

After all these years of loneliness I have found my long-lost mother, Geoffrey-Geoffrey thought, *and now I would like to kill her.*

'My son,' said the Hearse Whisperer, trying to pretend she cared as she wondered how long she would have to wait until she could lose him again.

'Mother,' said Geoffrey-Geoffrey, doing a pretty good impersonation of a loving son as he wondered how long he would have to wait before he could rip her head off.

'Yes, yes, very touching,' sneered Countess Slab. 'But you can't stay here. There's barely enough room for the two of us.'

Ex-King Quatorze took his wife to one side

142

and explained who the Hearse Whisperer was. He told the Countess that she had been his chief spy and was just about the most evil being in the whole world. He suggested that if there was ever going to be any way the two of them could get off Rockall, the Hearse Whisperer could be the creature most likely to help them.

'Well, I think they should go back to where they came from,' said the Countess.

'I was thinking that too,' said Geoffrey-Geoffrey, who had happened to overhear their conversation. 'Go back along the drain that brought me here.'

'Drain?' said the Hearse Whisperer. 'There's a drain?'

'Oh yes, of course!' cried Countess Slab. 'We can escape this hell-hole at last.'

'No,' said Geoffrey-Geoffrey, 'you can't. You're much too fat to fit in the drain.'

He pointed at Ex-King Quatorze. 'And so are you,' he added.

'Well, yes, OK, maybe,' said the Ex-King. 'You, my good and faithful servant, my dear old friend

Hearse Whisperer, you can go and, as soon as you are free, you can bring back a boat to rescue us.'

'And once we return to Transylvania Waters,' he continued, 'we will reclaim the throne, and you will be incredibly well rewarded.'

'How well?'

'Incredibly well.'

'Can I have your daughter's liver on toast?' said the Hearse Whisperer.

'Umm, er . . .' Ex-King Quatorze began.

Countess Slab gave him an enormous kick, and when he was then pulled out of the sea Quatorze said, 'Of course you can.'

'Then we will return with a boat and rescue you,' said the Hearse Whisperer. 'And if you do not keep your part of the bargain, it will be bits of you on toast, very, very delicate bits, and the rest of you will be kept alive to watch me eat them.'

Geoffrey-Geoffrey squeezed himself back into the drain and was followed by his mother.

'You go first,' she had said, determined not to have her son behind her, where she couldn't see

what he was doing. 'After all, you know the way.'

'But there is only one way,' Geoffrey-Geoffrey had said, very nervous to have his mother behind him, where he couldn't see what she was doing.

Either way it made no difference. It was so dark in the tunnel, neither of them could see anything.

Unfortunately, Gruinard had just turned off her tracking equipment about thirty seconds before Geoffrey-Geoffrey squeezed back into the tunnel, so none of them knew he was on his way back.

There was an alarm built into the system but, as luck would have it, an earthquake in Patagonia had sent a shockwave right around the world that had made a small crack appear in the Fruit-Pulp Pool drain, allowing several very hungry cockroaches into the drain. They wriggled through a small construction hole, which the builders should have sealed off but had forgotten to, and into the main wiring conduit that led across to Gruinard's secret cellar of wonderful machines.

And, of course, the first wire the cockroaches chewed through was the one that controlled the alarm.

The second wire they wrecked was the one that controlled the Broken-Alarm-Safety-Backup-Alarm-alarm.

So basically no one had the faintest idea that Geoffrey-Geoffrey and the Hearse Whisperer were on their way back up the drains.

Being in total darkness, their progress was slow. Mother and son had to feel their way along, which meant poking their fingers into lots of things they were very glad they couldn't see. Some of these unmentionable things made whimpering noises. Some growled. Some tried to bite their fingers off and all of them smelled slightly worse than a bucket of brussels sprouts that had been fermenting for a month in the bottom of the terrifying sewer that ran under the Diarrhoea Research Institute of Ghent.

Actually, the sewer didn't so much run as limp along very slowly, forever getting more and more stagnant. Even the Hearse Whisperer, who had seen

147

it all, eaten it all, killed it all, torn all its limbs off and squashed it all,[45] found it hard not to throw up. The accompanying fumes made her eyelashes melt and run down her face.

Geoffrey-Geoffrey had lost his sense of smell in a small Belgian coffee shop one Saturday afternoon. He had reported the loss to the police and said that he'd had his sense of smell when he had gone into the cafe, but at some point he had lost it and no amount of searching could locate it.

'I can only assume that someone stole it,' he had said.

Now, discovering how much his mother was suffering, he was rather glad he hadn't found his sense of smell. But he too couldn't ignore the fumes, which were melting his hair and making it run down his body to his feet so that his toes stuck together.

All this hardship only made mother and son even more determined to get their revenge on the Floods.

---

[45] *Though not necessarily in that order.*

'We will make their lives so unbearable that they will wish they were dead, but instead of making them dead,' the Hearse Whisperer said, 'we will then make them feel better and all happy again and in love with the whole world. Then we will kill them.'

'How will we do it, Mother?' said Geoffrey-Geoffrey, realising that when it came to being evil, he still had so much to learn.

I have always prided myself on my evilness, he thought, *but next to my mother I am a mere amateur.*

He hadn't changed his mind about taking revenge on his mother for how she had discarded him and ruined his life, but first he would make sure he learned every vile, cruel, heartless thing he could from her.

Then I shall kill her, he thought, smiling to himself.

Stupid child, thought the Hearse Whisperer. *He thinks to pick my brain and take all the evil it has taken me years to perfect. He thinks then to kill me, but I shall be ready, and in the split second before he does it, I shall kill him and eat him on toast.*

149

Meanwhile, Nerlin and Quenelle had gone back down the path to her cave, although it had taken a lot of persuading to get him to leave the Valley of the Impossible Waterfall.

Gruinard had let Nerlin mark out the place where he wanted to build his retirement cottage. It stood on its own around a bend in the river, set back from the water. Wildflowers in every colour of the rainbow grew there, among soft bushes and grass as lush as velvet. Nerlin couldn't wait to dig it all up and build his cottage.

'I will come back as soon as I can,' he had said. 'Once I have retired and young Valla is crowned King.'

He wasn't entirely convinced that his eldest son Valla would actually take the job, even though he was the heir to the throne. Of course if Nerlin were to die then Valla would have no choice, but Nerlin thought he probably wouldn't enjoy living

in a beautiful cottage up in the lovely valley quite so much if he were dead. At least, not as much as he would if he were alive.

But I am the King, he thought. *Which means I'm in charge, and if Valla won't be King, then I'll make a law saying the next one down can have the job, whether it be my son or my daughter. On the other hand, the next eldest is Satanella, but then my people might not like being ruled over by a small dog, and that would mean Merlinmary, who I think scares quite a lot of people, would be next in line.*

Nerlin had never thought that not being King anymore would be so complicated. Winchflat spent most of the time on some other planet full of strange inventions, so he wouldn't want the job, and the twins would never be able to agree which one of them should wear the crown.

'So that leaves Betty,' he said. 'And, actually, I think she'd probably be the best at it.'

As he sat daydreaming about Betty's coronation and what a great party they could have with exciting food that was kept for special occasions, including

the legendary Poached Brussels Sprouts Dipped in Chocolate, someone touched him on the shoulder.

It was Anorexya.

'You look sad, Your Majesty,' she said softly.

Her hand stayed on Nerlin's shoulder and he became aware of a strange tingling feeling running down his arm. A warm glow spread throughout his whole body, making him forget all thoughts of not being king and who might do the job when he retired. It was a weird but nice sensation that he hadn't felt since he'd been a young man and it stirred long-forgotten feelings in a tiny room inside the back of his head.

They were nice feelings, so nice, in fact, that he found it quite easy to forget all the other things he had been thinking about, like going home to his wife and children and castle, and making plans for his retirement, including popping in to Burnings, the famous Transylvania Waters hardware store, to collect some colour charts to help him decide what shade to paint the window frames on the idyllic cottage he was going to build in the Valley of the Impossible Waterfall, where he and, um, er, Queen, er, what's-her-name, um, were going to retire.

He forgot all of that, even his beloved wife's name and the earache he had just got from the

wasp that had flown into his left ear.

For, as Anorexya had put her hand on Nerlin's shoulder, she had cast an Enchantment Spell[46] over him, and he was now like putty in her hands, and not like the hard, lumpy bits of putty used to seal window panes, but soft, new putty that Anorexya could mould into whatever shape she wanted.

She had but to suggest something, anything, and Nerlin would agree.

Only a few hours earlier, Transylvania Waters's poor King had been rescued from the Doolally Spell the evil Geoffrey-Geoffrey had cast on him that had made everyone think he was going senile. Now Anorexya had given him a new enchantment that had turned him into a labrador puppy. It's not that Nerlin looked like a puppy – he was just all gooey and dopey, so, actually, he was more like a spaniel than a labrador.

'You are not happy, are you, my beloved?' Anorexya said softly.

---

[46] *Which is like a Disenchantment Spell, only the complete opposite.*

Nerlin, now freed from Geoffrey-Geoffrey's Doolally Spell, had been quite happy with the promise of even being perfectly happy. He had been looking forward to going back to Dreary and into the arms of his loving family.

But now he was bewitched, and being bewitched by a witch is the strongest sort of bewitching, even more powerful than the combination of bacon and chocolate in a sandwich.

He looked up at Anorexya with his googly eyes and said in a soppy, baby voice, 'No, Nerlin is not happy. He has a sadness.'

'Do not worry, my beloved. Your darling, your one true, lovely Anorexya is here to take care of you,' said Anorexya. 'You'd like that, wouldn't you?'

'Yes.'

'We don't want to go back to that nasty Dreary, where it's all dark, and to that nasty Castle Twilight full of slime and damp, do we?'

'No, we don't want to go there,' said Nerlin. 'We would get covered in mould and slugs.'

'That's right,' said Anorexya. 'No, we will stay

right away from there and go to the far end of the world, to the land of my ancestors in Patagonia. We will go high up into the mountains to Shangrila Lakes, and there we will eat enchanted cakes and buns and drink fizzy pop, not the ordinary kind, but magical fizzy pop that flows like nectar from the Fountain of Eternal Youth.'

'Wow,' said Nerlin. 'Nerlin loves fizzy pop.'

'Yes, I know you do,' Anorexya said to herself. 'I've done the research.'

Then she said out loud, 'And it will be strawberry-flavoured fizzy pop. Your favourite.'

'Yes,' said Nerlin. 'And Nerlin likes eternal youth too.'

'Well, who doesn't?' said Anorexya, and she clicked her fingers – the finger clicking was just for effect because at the same time she pressed a red button on a remote control – and a hot-air balloon floated from within the clouds to stop right in front of Nerlin, hovering a couple of metres above the grass.

A skinny little man with very bad skin and

a runny nose appeared from inside the basket. He threw a rope ladder over the side and climbed down.

'Step aboard, Your Majesty,' he said, bowing low so his nose dripped all over his feet.

'Yes,' Anorexya murmured. 'Climb aboard, my beloved, and we shall whisk you away to eternal happiness.'

The balloon rose up into the sky just as Quenelle came out of her cave to tell Nerlin that tea was ready. Of course by then he wasn't there, but something made her look up just in time to see the last little bit of the balloon's mooring rope vanish into the clouds.

'Anorexya, Dispepsya,' she called out. 'Come quick. Someone has kidnapped the King!'

'Where? Who? What?' called Dispepsya, running out of her cave, almost dropping the cup in her hands. 'Oops, I've spilt my tea.'

Up in the cloud, Anorexya heard Quenelle shouting and laughed.

Under the cloud, Quenelle heard Anorexya laughing and realised what had happened. Anorexya had always had a twinkle in her eye whenever Nerlin had been around. She had always run back into her cave and changed into her best rags and sprinkled herself with enchanted ditch water and become all giggly.[47]

All the other Old Crones knew that Anorexya had a crush on Nerlin, but none of them had ever expected she would do anything about it apart from a lot of blushing and carving his name on her shins with her machete.

Anorexya's laughter grew fainter and fainter as the balloon rose higher and higher, clearing the clouds as it floated towards Patagonia. Then it was gone, taking Nerlin and his kidnappers with it.

'Thank goodness I came out in time,' said

---

[47] *An ancient, wrinkly Old Crone being giggly sounds a bit like a chainsaw with a lot of teeth missing trying to cut its way through a bucket of rusty nails.*

Quenelle. 'Another minute and the rope would have vanished and we would have had no idea what'd happened.'

'Except Anorexya would have vanished too,' said Dispepsya.

'Yes, but she often goes off into the forest to eat millipedes, and sometimes we don't see her for weeks,' said one of the other crones.

'Right,' said Quenelle. 'Fetch my mobile. I'll ring Castle Twilight and tell them what's happened. The sooner we go after them the better.'

'Where's your mobile?' said Dispepsya.

'On the shelf, above the number six cauldron,' said Quenelle. 'We all keep our mobiles there.'

'I know,' said Dispepsya, 'but they aren't there.'

'What, none of them?'

'No.'

A quick search of high, followed by a long search of low, followed by another more careful search of high and low revealed nothing. Every single one of the Old Crones' mobiles had vanished.

Anorexya had planned the kidnap very

159

efficiently. There was a single landline phone down to Dreary and she had cut that too, in dozens of places. And finally, she had pulled all the feathers out of the wings of Fluffy Sainte-Marie the carrier pigeon.

The only way to get news to Mordonna and the others was for someone to go down the footpath.

'What about the broomsticks?' someone suggested. 'One of us could fly down on one of them.'

'Except we got rid of them all when we got the vacuum cleaners,' said Quenelle.

'I could fly down on one of them,' said Slandarella, who was not actually an Old Crone, but the lumpy older sister of one of them who they had employed out of charity. Slandarella made the tea, did the washing up and made sure everyone had enough boils and scabs.

Luckily, one of the donkeys had been left behind for Nerlin when Mordonna and everyone else had gone back to Dreary, so it was agreed that Dispepsya would ride it to the castle and get help.

Meanwhile, the hot-air balloon rose up through the clouds until Nerlin and Anorexya were drifting far above them. The pilot turned off the seatbelt sign and pulled on the ropes until their course was set for Patagonia.

Anorexya fed Nerlin fizzy pop, enchanted cakes

and buns with added sleeping pills and soon the King was drifting, not just through the stratosphere, but through a vast library of dreams that Anorexya had manufactured. Many of the happiest memories of his life that involved times spent with Mordonna were replaced with fake memories of days spent with Anorexya.

They drifted south-west across France, over Spain and out to sea, and when they were hundreds of miles away from land, Anorexya threw the Old Crones' mobiles over the side. Amazingly, their fall towards the sea was interrupted by a lone pelican, who swallowed one of the phones.

Nerlin slept like a baby. Not one of those babies that wet the bed and have nightmares, but the ones that sleep all through the night without a peep and don't actually exist.

The balloon reached South America and sailed south-west towards Patagonia.

Anorexya couldn't believe she had got away with it. Everything had gone perfectly and it wasn't as if she'd spent years planning everything. In fact,

she'd only had the few days since Nerlin and everyone had come up to the caves.

Of course, it wouldn't take long for the Old Crones to realise that she had disappeared at the same time as Nerlin, but it would take ages for them to work out where they had gone. Anorexya was pretty sure that no one knew she came from Shangrila Lakes. After all, hardly anyone even knew the place existed.

Once there, she would get Nerlin's marriage to Mordonna declared illegal and she would become Mrs Flood. And after she disposed of her father, the King of Shangrila Lakes, and her brother, Prince Bert, who was the heir to the throne, she and Nerlin would become the King and Queen of Shangrila Lakes.

'And we will live happily ever after,' she said to herself, 'especially after he gets cosmetic surgery.'

Except everything had not gone completely perfectly. There had been the little bit of rope hanging out of the cloud.

If Quenelle had come out her cave two minutes later, or if she had come at the right time but not looked up, then Anorexya would have got clean away.

Although the rope didn't tell Quenelle where they had gone, it did tell her that Nerlin had been taken away by balloon and Anorexya's laughter coming down through the clouds had told her who had taken him. Quenelle racked her brains to try to work out where they would be heading. There were several possibilities:[48]

- **Tristan da Cunha** – *This was top of the list. Even with the fastest magic available, it would take days to get there, but its remoteness made it a perfect hiding place.* On the other hand,

---

[48] *There were over fifteen million possibilities, but Quenelle refused to let herself think that.*

Quenelle thought, its remoteness makes it hard to escape from.

- **Belgium** – *This was the most unlikely place and therefore one of the most likely. Anorexya was the sort of person who could easily take Nerlin there, just for the hell of it.* On the other hand, *Quenelle thought,* its unlikeliness makes it quite likely. Or not.

- **Transylvania Waters** – *This was also very unlikely, while being the perfect place, so therefore likely. There were hundreds of caves hidden up in the mountains, even little secret valleys perfect for concealing a kidnapped king.* But then what would Anorexya do? *Quenelle thought.* She would hardly be satisfied keeping Nerlin hidden away. She would want the world to know he was hers.

It was all very difficult. The world was a huge place and there were just so many possibilities. By the time she had finished writing them down, Quenelle had a list of over fifty.

And none of them was Shangrila Lakes.

Dispepsya stood at the top of the narrow slippery path that led down to the valley. Crème-de-Menthe, the donkey who was going to carry her, was in a bad mood and not just the standard bad mood that most donkeys are in, but a special bad mood that only a really stuck-up, snobby donkey could get into.

'Are you King Nerlin?' Crème-de-Menthe said. 'The noble ruler of our magnificent country? Of course you're not. You're just a lumpy, ugly Old Crone and not even the top Old Crone. Was I brought up here to carry you down to Dreary? Of course I wasn't. I mean, if someone had said to me, "Excuse me, oh wonderful donkey, would you please drag yourself up a slippery rocky path to some godforsaken cave and fetch a smelly old woman back here?" what do you think I would have said?'

Crème-de-Menthe then told anyone who

would listen what she would have said and it included fifteen of the most disgusting words ever created.

'I mean,' Crème-de-Menthe continued, 'I am not just any donkey, you know. I have twice been voted Miss Beautiful Hooves in the Dreary Annual Show and I was runner-up in *Transylvania Waters's Got Talent* for my beautiful performance of Elton John's "Goodbye Yellow Thick Toad". I am someone to be reckoned with, you know.'

'Indeed you are,' said Quenelle. 'And that is why you have been personally chosen to carry the messenger down to our glorious Queen Mordonna, to let her know that our magnificent ruler, the Awesome King Nerlin, has been kidnapped.'

'Oh,' said Crème-de-Menthe. 'I suppose that's different, then.'

'It is indeed,' said Quenelle. 'Why, I wouldn't be surprised if the Queen rewards you in a most magnificent way. You could even get the Golden Carrot Award.'

'Really?'

'Absolutely.'

'OK,' said Crème-de-Menthe. 'Is there any chance you could hose the Old Crone down before we set off, though? I mean, she does smell dreadful, and if there is one thing us donkeys know a lot about, it's stinky things.'

Dispepsya was not about to take a bath.

'After all,' she protested, 'I haven't got to where I am today by washing.'

'That, I think everyone would agree, is obvious,' said Crème-de-Menthe. 'Didn't you have a bath in the Fruit-Pulp Pool?'

'Yes and no,' said Dispepsya. 'I'm like a duck. Water rolls off me without having any effect at all. Some people think it's part of my charm.'

'So even if we did hose you off it wouldn't make any difference,' said Crème-de-Menthe. 'You'd still be a horrible, stinky old woman.'

'Listen, pony,' Dispepsya snapped, well aware that the greatest insult you can throw at a donkey is to call it a pony, 'if I were to go out into the middle of the densest forest on earth and get lost, my unique scent would lead my rescuers to me in no time at all.'

'Are you likely to go out into the middle of the densest forest on earth?' said Crème-de-Menthe.

'Well, no . . .' Dispepsya began.

'Pity.'

'OK, you two,' said Quenelle. 'Enough with the arguing. Just get down the mountain before our beloved King is taken so far away we will never be able to find him. You should be ashamed of yourselves.'

She clipped a big clothes peg on the donkey's nose to keep out the smell, but because Crème-de-Menthe was chewing a huge mouthful of grass and couldn't breathe through her mouth, she fainted.

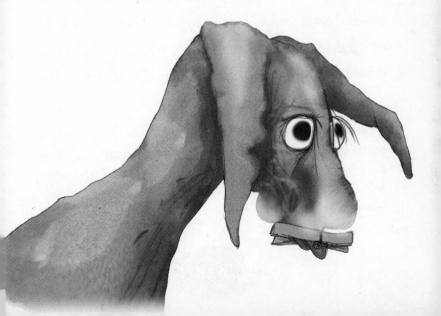

'And I could even smell her when I was unconscious,' said the donkey, when they'd removed the clothes peg and brought her round again.

In the end Quenelle tied a big bunch of lavender under the donkey's nose, which hid the Old Crone's smell a bit as they set off down towards home.

Their beloved King had been taken as far as he was going.

The balloon had passed unseen over Quicklime College, traversed the frozen mountains and hills beyond, and come gently down to earth in a field of bright green grass at the edge of Shangrila Lakes' only lake.[49] At the other end of the lake was the

---

[49] *Considering Shangrila Lakes was called Shangrila Lakes, it was a bit strange that it actually only had the one lake. There were lots of streams and a few puddles, but no more lakes or even ponds. But Shangrila Lakes' one lake was very, very lovely and seriously enchanted.*

country's only town, but where Anorexya and Nerlin had landed was peaceful, private and quiet. A single enchanted cottage sat in a secret garden of beautiful flowers a mere ten metres from the water's edge.

Anorexya had emailed ahead so that when she arrived everything was ready. Nerlin, still sleeping, was carried into the cottage, where he was dressed in beautiful velvet robes. Around his wrists and ankles were shackles of the finest gold, joined together by deceptively strong chains.

'Just in case,' Anorexya said to her two maid servants.

No one, apart from her two maid servants and Old Wobbly the gardener, knew that Princess Anorexya had returned to the land of her birth. Everyone knew that she had left many years ago because of some terrible naughtiness that no one would talk about. Since then, most people had forgotten she even existed.

Anorexya was well aware of this and that was one reason she had kidnapped Nerlin and brought him to Shangrila Lakes. Not only had she come

home, but she had brought the world's top wizard with her,[50] and she was going to marry him and they would be the King and Queen of Shangrila Lakes, and all those people who had driven her away with their revolting accusations would be seriously and painfully sorry. The fact that every single one of those accusations was true was completely irrelevant.

For now, she would lie low while the worldwide panic over Nerlin's disappearance reached its peak and then began to fade away. This could take a while, but that would not be wasted time. Anorexya knew that the wretched genius Winchflat Flood would probably have implanted everyone in the family with tracking devices in case they did get kidnapped, but he wasn't the only evil genius in the world.

She had already made contact with Dr Atrocius Strabismus, the evil twin brother of the famous

---

[50] *Calling Nerlin the world's top wizard does not in any way mean that he was the world's best wizard. As we have seen in earlier Floods books, he was actually pretty useless at magic, but he was the King of Transylvania Waters and that made him Top Wizard.*

Professor Nylon Strabismus, and he was on his way from his mountain lair in Austria to scan Nerlin and remove any devices. He would then implant the device in an albatross and send it on its way.

In the meantime she would keep the king sedated and inactive.

The great advantage in using Dr Atrocius was that he was also a highly skilled plastic surgeon and would be able to transform Nerlin into anyone Anorexya wanted.

She had a big collage on her bedroom wall of all the best bits from the world's best blokes – ancient and modern. Knees from one, blue eyes from another, muscles from the greatest athlete of all time, armpits from a 1930s movie star and so on. Every day she went through countless books and magazines, cutting out bits of pictures and updating and improving the image of her dream man.

Nerlin would be perfect and he would be all hers.

13

$\mathcal{A}$fter twenty-three long, slow and exhausting hours, Crème-de-Menthe with Dispepsya asleep on her back staggered into Castle Twilight.

'Halt, who goes there?' said the castle guard.

'It's me, you idiot,' said Crème-de-Menthe. 'You can see who I am, and I've got this Old Crone on my back.'

'All I can see,' said the guard, 'is a clapped-out old donkey with a bag of rags and bones on its back.'

'Listen, stupid, we have to see the Queen and it's urgent.'

'Oh yes? They all say that,' said the guard. 'You could at least try to be a bit more original.'

'If you don't let us see the Queen right away,'

said Crème-de-Menthe, 'you will be seriously sorry and probably spend the rest of your life cleaning the castle lavatories with your tongue.'

'They all say that too,' the guard replied. 'Why, if I had a dolor for every time I've heard that, I'd be a rich man.'

Crème-de-Menthe decided to try another approach. She turned around and kicked the guard as hard as she could, which, being a donkey with very powerful back legs, was very hard indeed.

'They all try that too,' groaned the guard, as he lay on the ground in agony.

Just as Crème-de-Menthe was about to step over the now unconscious guard, Betty, who had popped out to get a takeaway cafe latte from Scarebutts, the coffee shop opposite the castle gates, came up.

'What's going on here?' she said, and Crème-de-Menthe explained.

'You are a great and noble donkey,' said Betty. 'I suggest you tip the old bag off your back and I will take you to my mother and you can tell her everything.'

175

Crème-de-Menthe shook herself and Dispepsya fell off onto the guard.[51]

When Mordonna heard that Nerlin had been kidnapped, she summoned her children and broke the news.

'Your poor father,' she said. 'He is such an innocent and trusting soul.'

'And I must tell you, your amazingly wonderful Highness,' said Crème-de-Menthe, 'that I think he had been done over with an Enchantment Spell by one of the Old Crones.'

'Are you sure?'

'Yes, my lady. I was standing behind a camellia bush, having a bit of a browse, when I heard her talking to the King,' Crème-de-Menthe explained.

---

[51] *Dispepsya and the castle guard slept for about four hours. When they finally woke up, they got to their feet, both blushing profusely, fell deeply in love with each other, got married, had fourteen children and lived happily ever after in a rather nice hovel, where they spent the rest of their lives carving rude sculptures out of turnips, which they sold to tourists at vastly inflated prices. There is even talk of an exhibition at a top New York gallery.*

'Then a balloon came down and took them away.'

'Right,' said Mordonna. 'So first of all we need to find out which Old Crone it was. That might give us a clue to where she's taken my poor darling.'

'It was Anorexya what done it, Your Highness,' said Crème-de-Menthe.

Winchflat was sent to get his Dad-Tracker. But the batteries were flat and no one could find a single replacement anywhere in the entire castle. So they had to wait forty-three minutes until the newsagent on the corner opened, only to find that the store had completely sold out of that particular battery and wasn't expecting any more stock until Friday and he wasn't actually sure which Friday.

So they went for the caves and told Quenelle to come down to the castle as soon as possible and that made the Old Crone faint because she hadn't been in the valley for over eighty years and was terrified she would get depth-sickness because of the extra oxygen at lower levels. Winchflat then had to make her a vacuum mask to suck the surplus air out of her lungs for her trip to Dreary.

All in all, the delays and interruptions wasted two days, neither of which were a Friday, so they still had no batteries. By then, Quenelle had been fitted with her vacuum mask that had been sent up to her by carrier goose, which is like a carrier pigeon but with a greater carrying capacity. Quenelle had then come down to Dreary and told Mordonna the little she knew.

Winchflat put on a white coat and told Quenelle he was a doctor while he used a stethoscope to listen to her breathing.

'I can assure you, dear lady,' he said, 'that you can remove your mask with absolute safety.'

What he didn't tell her was that the mask was a complete fake anyway.

'Oooh, I feel quite heavy-headed,' she said, and then told Mordonna about Anorexya.

'So where does she come from?' Mordonna asked. 'It might give us a clue to where she is.'

'I don't know,' said Quenelle. 'She just appeared at our caves one morning.'

'And she's never told you anything about her past?'

'No, not a single word.'

'Didn't you think that was odd?' said Mordonna.

'Well, yes, but then most of us Old Crones have secrets from our pasts that we keep to ourselves,' Quenelle explained. 'It's an unwritten rule that we never ask each other about our pasts. Of course, some of us are only too happy to talk about our previous lives, but others, like Anorexya, keep everything hidden away.'

She showed everyone her list of the most likely places Anorexya might have taken Nerlin. Phone calls were made, texts and emails sent, but they all came up blank, even Tristan da Cunha, which Mordonna thought the most likely.

Eventually, someone found two batteries and they all sat around Winchflat's Dad-Tracker.

'According to this,' Winchflat said, 'Father is gliding across a huge open ocean, kilometres from anywhere.'

'So they're still travelling in the balloon then,' said Betty.

'That's what I thought, but then Father rose into the air before diving beneath the waves and catching a mackerel,' said Winchflat. 'In fact, he keeps doing it. I reckon he's swallowed about twenty-five of them.'

He consulted an app on his wPhone[52] called the iFish-Capacity-Ometer, which told him that an adult male wizard could eat no more than four mackerel and the only creature living where the Dad-Tracker sensor currently was would be an albatross.

'Oh my God!' Mordonna cried. 'My beloved husband has been swallowed by an albatross.'

'That's just physically impossible, Mother,' said Winchflat. 'No, it means that the sensor and Father have parted ways, and whoever removed it has fed it to the giant bird.'

'Do you mean they've cut my darling open?' Mordonna cried.

'Well, yes, but it's a really tiny device,' said Winchflat. 'It would only be a very small cut. What intrigues me, though, is who might have done it.

---

[52] *Which is an iPhone for wizards.*

There are very few people in the world who would have the technical ability to detect such a sensor.'

'How many people?' said Betty.

Winchflat thought about it. Several times he held up his hand as though he had come up with an answer, only to put it down again a minute later.

'Now that I think about it,' he said, 'there is only one person. He is the evil twin of my old friend Professor Nylon Strabismus, and his name is Dr Atrocius Strabismus. He is the only person who would have the skills to do such a thing.'

'OK, so where do we find him?' said Mordonna.

'Well, like all evil mad scientists, he lives in a remote mountain-top retreat in Austria,' said Winchflat. 'I will call his brother and see if he knows where he is.'

Mordonna had a strong feeling that she knew where Nerlin had been taken. She decided to wait and see what Professor Strabismus told them before she said anything, because it was such a secret place that less than a dozen people who didn't live there knew about. It was so secret that quite a lot of people who did live there didn't even know about it.

Shangrila Lakes.

She didn't know why, but the feeling that Nerlin had been taken there grew stronger and stronger.

When Winchflat got hold of the professor, he couldn't tell them where his brother had gone.

'But I am know zat he haf avay gone no milks for now,' the professor said, which is Austrian for, 'But I do know he's gone away because he has stopped the milk.'

However, he did suggest that extracting some DNA from Anorexya's clothes might give them a clue, and sure enough a pair of her old bloomers, which Winchflat put in his Jeans-n-Genes Scanner, showed that she came from a very ancient and obscure family that drew a complete blank when he searched for it on his database.

'That's impossible,' he said.

'What does the scanner say?' Mordonna asked.

'SL000 type 0001,' Winchflat replied. 'Which indicates that it's from several million years before the records began. If I wasn't seeing the numbers in

183

front of me, I would say that they were impossible.'

'SL000?' said Mordonna. 'I'm pretty sure I know what that means, and if I'm right, then I know where your father has been taken.'

'Really?' said Winchflat, seriously impressed that his mother might have some scientific information he knew nothing about.

'Yes,' said Mordonna. 'SL – Shangrila Lakes.'

'It sounds like a retirement village,' said Betty.

'It's a country.'

Winchflat typed and googled and typed some more, but nothing came up.

'Are you sure?' he said. 'There's not a single mention of it anywhere on the net.'

'No,' said Mordonna, 'nor will you find it anywhere in any book. It's sort of like here, only much, much smaller. It was where a branch of our family called the Creaks set up a new kingdom several hundred years ago, when they thought Transylvania Waters was getting far too friendly with the world of humans and they were worried that our magical powers would get diluted by them.'

'So how come you're the only person who knows about it?' said Betty.

'Because they have a Perpetual Secrecy Spell, which blankets the world so no one can ever find them,' Mordonna explained. 'The only reason I found out about it is because when I was very young they tried to persuade me to go live there and marry my fifty-fourth cousin, who was the heir to the Shangrila Lakes throne.'

'But what makes you think our father is there?' said Winchflat.

'Well, if the DNA test shows that Anorexya comes from there, then I reckon it would be the perfect place for her to take him,' said Mordonna. 'After all, no one knows where it actually is.'

Now in the same way a tiny event had shown everyone that Nerlin had been taken away in a balloon, another tiny event came to them as a clue to where Shangrila Lakes might be.

As the balloon had flown over Quicklime College, Nerlin had coughed and twitched in his sleep. His feet had shot up in the air and, before

Anorexya could grab it, his left boot had slipped off his foot and fallen through the clouds, landing on a small boy called Phoebus Sandal, the youngest son of the famous wizard family the Sandals of Trembleton. It just so happened that the Sandal family were owners of Transylvania Waters's finest and only vineyard, famous throughout wizardom for its Cabinet-Savage-Blank wine, a wine that was so powerful two glasses could make you forget, umm, er, whatsit.

The boot had knocked poor Phoebus unconscious, though when it was realised that the boot had belonged to King Nerlin, it was considered a great honour. An email was sent from Quicklime College to Castle Twilight, asking Nerlin if he wanted his boot back.

Within two hours Mordonna had organised the Quicklime's dragon school bus to pick up the Floods from Transylvania Waters and whisk them around the world to the college, where Winchflat had fed all the available information into his laptop and calculated from the direction and angle of the

boot's trajectory which way the balloon must have been flying.

'But there's nothing there,' said everyone at the college. 'It's just endless lines of valleys and mountains buried in ice and snow. Nothing lives there except vultures, and they're half-starved most of the time.'

'Maybe there's a secret cave buried deep in one of the mountains,' said Winchflat, though when he went to the far end of Quicklime's valley and scanned as far ahead as he could, there was no evidence of anything, except for the ice, snow, three emaciated vultures, and the long-lost wreckage of a plane full of Belgian geography teachers, who even the vultures had refused to eat.

'There's nothing there,' Winchflat reported. 'We've been led on a wild-boot chase. We might as well go home.'

But then a report came from a fourth vulture, which had been found unconscious in the next valley with Nerlin's other boot lying beside him. When the vulture was carried back to the school and revived, it spoke of a large balloon flying high overhead.

'Heading west, it was,' said the vulture, 'and when I flew up to investigate, someone threw that boot at me.'

'Did you see who was in the balloon?' said Mordonna.

'No,' the vulture replied. 'The boot hit me on the head when I was about twenty metres below the basket, so all I saw were stars and the ground coming up very fast. Then I passed out.'

The scraggy bird was given a very dead and very fat rat, as well as a warm cup of blood and woodlice, before it was sent happily on its way.

'But there's nothing there,' said Winchflat.

'Maybe your equipment is faulty,' Betty suggested, but Winchflat insisted he had tested, checked and double-checked it all and everything was working fine.

'It's the Perpetual Secrecy Spell,' said Mordonna. 'It's like an invisible lead cloak that hides the country from the world. I've never been there, so I don't know for certain what it's like, but I was told that the place was like a miniature version of Transylvania Waters.'

NOTHING TO SEE

HERE

OR HERE

'So, what you're saying is that in one of the hundreds of snow-filled frozen valleys between here and the sea, hidden beneath this spell, is Shangrila Lakes?' said Winchflat.

'Yes,' said Mordonna.

'You're absolutely sure of that?'

'No, but have you got any other ideas?' said Mordonna.

'They could have gone on beyond South America,' said Winchflat. 'They could be on the Galapagos Islands.'

'No, too many people,' said Mordonna.

'And our agent there says no one new has arrived for over a fortnight.'

'OK,' said Winchflat. 'Let's assume you're right. How do we find out which is the right valley? There are hundreds of them.'

They wrote down their options, which included:

- *Melt all the ice and snow in every valley. The only trouble was that this would probably flood millions of people's homes all around the world due to the rise in sea level, and Shangrila Lakes would still be hidden by the Perpetual Secrecy Spell.*

- *Try to reverse the spell, and then use that to create a We Can See You Spell. The trouble with this one was that it could take forever to do, seeing as they had no idea how the Perpetual Secrecy Spell had been created in the first place. All they knew was that it was perpetual and that it was full of secrecy and that it was a spell.*

- *Create a machine that could detect heartbeats*

even through a Perpetual Secrecy Spell. The problem with this was that the machine would need to be so powerful that it would pick up the heartbeats of every ant and every worm in every valley.

'Well, I'm stumped,' said Winchflat, feeling quite upset that he couldn't think of a way to bypass or neutralise the spell.

'There is another solution,' said Betty.

'I don't think there is, little sister,' said Winchflat.

'Money,' said Betty. 'Just let it be known that we will pay a huge reward for the GPS co-ordinates of Shangrila Lakes.'

Even Winchflat agreed that was a great idea. Within an hour the reward was being advertised on every wizard bulletin board and blog around the world, and within one hour and one minute, emails were pouring in.

Still certain that Shangrila Lakes was somewhere beyond Quicklime College in deepest Patagonia, the

Floods set up camp at the school. Winchflat created a quick computer program to analyse and correlate the emails.

Most of the messages were just guesses, some ridiculous, some rude, and most were wildly inaccurate. Ninety-nine-point-nine-nine percent of them had come from people who had never heard of Shangrila Lakes, with many just saying outright that there was no such place.

Winchflat's software worked in both directions and everyone who sent a nasty email discovered that the computer and/or mobile they had used to send the message was suddenly able to do an incredible impersonation of a small bonfire. Lots of things all over the world caught fire, not just phones and computers, but in some cases, the houses, cars and trouser pockets they had been stored in were set ablaze too.

Naturally, several paranoid governments claimed the fires were due to dangerous terrorists and began wasting yet even more money on pointless and useless things they called 'Security Measures'.

Winchflat had guessed this would happen and his computer program made sure that the 'Security Measures' caught on fire too.

By the time the word had got around and people had stopped sending in emails, Winchflat had saved three that actually looked as if they could be useful.

The first one was from someone who'd said his father's uncle's best friend had run a delivery service, and had delivered twelve kilos of treacle toffee to an old wizard living in a place called Shangrila Lakes in 1923. He thought that the postal address might still be in the glove box of the delivery van. The trouble was that when his father's uncle's best friend had died in 1957, he had been buried in the delivery van in a graveyard somewhere near Stockholm, which was now the site of a twenty-seven-storey block of flats. Winchflat put this email at the bottom of the pile of three.

The second one was from someone who'd said his mother's aunt's niece had run a delivery service, and in 1925 and again in 1926 and 1927

she'd delivered twelve kilos of treacle toffee to an old wizard living in a place called Shangrila Lakes. Apparently she had got the job when the previous delivery service had put their prices up. He thought that the postal address might still be in the door pocket of the delivery van, which was now in a Delivery Van Museum on the ground floor of a twenty-seven-storey office block, allegedly built

above an old graveyard in downtown Stockholm. Winchflat put this email on top of the first one.

The third email was from Anorexya. It said, in very rude, sarcastic words, that there was no way they would ever find her because they were useless and obsolete and stupid, whereas she was brilliant and clever and getting more beautiful every minute, and anyway Nerlin was in love with her and never wanted to see Mordonna or any of his horrible, gross, stupid children again, and besides Transylvania Waters was rubbish and nowhere as incredible as Shangrila Lakes, which was the top wizard place in the entire universe, and once she and Nerlin were married and became King and Queen they would sell Transylvania Waters to Belgium for fifteen scents, and all the witches and wizards who lived there would have their powers removed by the Grand Council and be reduced to ordinary, useless humans who would have to spend the rest of their lives polishing turnips in the worst market in Brussels.

'Grand Council?' Mordonna texted. 'What Grand Council?'

'THE Grand Council,' Anorexya texted back. 'The one I am in charge of. The Grand Council that must be obeyed by everyone or else.'

Just in case Anorexya had a bug in the room, which of course she didn't, Winchflat wrote on a piece of paper for them to keep texting Anorexya while he tracked down the signal that would tell them where she was hiding.

'Or else what?' Mordonna texted.

'You'll see,' texted Anorexya. 'And don't think you can keep texting me while that stupid so-called clever son of your tries to track my location. Shangrila Lakes has a cloaking device that makes it undetectable.'

'So you're in Shangrila Lakes then?' Mordonna wrote.

'Umm, no, umm, of course not,' Anorexya texted back while kicking herself.

'And besides,' Mordonna texted, 'we know that your full name is Anorexya Disinfectant Creak and that you are the daughter of the king of Shangrila Lakes. So it seems very likely that's where you are.'

'You're just full of hot air, stupid smelly hot air that stinks like it came out of a pig's bottom,' Betty texted. 'And on top of that, Shangrila Lakes is rubbish. I've seen prettier rubbish dumps. And it's tiny and we are going to come and turn everyone who lives there into small dogs with rotten teeth and bad breath.'

'Oh yeah?' Anorexya replied. 'You and whose army?'

'We don't need an army,' Betty texted. 'The assistant gardener's grandmother's old dog Neephus could beat you up with one paw tied behind her back.'

After two more minutes of backwards-and-forwards abuse, Winchflat gave a thumbs up. Betty called Anorexya a pig's bum and turned off her mobile.

'Shangrila Lakes is about eighty kilometres from here,' said Winchflat. 'If we use the dragon bus, we could get there in less than an hour.'

'If I'm not mistaken,' said Mordonna, 'doesn't Quicklime College have a class in building missiles?'

197

'It does indeed,' said Winchflat.

They sent for Seldom Hairpeace, the school's weapons master, and together he and Winchflat designed a special missile that would be sent to Shangrila Lakes ten minutes before dawn, to be followed by the school bus ten minutes later.

Naturally, the missile was not designed to kill or maim.[53] It took three hours to arm the missile, which was then fitted with a computer-controlled guidance system, and at a quarter to dawn, Betty lit the touchpaper. As the missile soared over the valleys and mountains, it left a trail of melted snow behind it, and once the missile was directly above Shangrila Lakes, it exploded with a massive bang that was heard right around the world.

---

[53] *Well, it was designed to maim a little bit, but only in a very sticky and embarrassing way.*

As soon as the missile exploded, the Floods got into the school bus and followed its trail. They stopped in front of a castle and climbed out to a scene of devastation.

Every single square inch of every single thing – people, animals, plants, furniture, houses – was covered in a thick layer of congealed porridge. The explosion had been so powerful that it had blown all the windows and doors in and covered everything inside with porridge too.

The porridge was a special Transylvania Waters recipe, which had been used for torturing prisoners in the good old days. Unlike normal porridge, this one set hard like treacle toffee. There were usually

enough holes in the porridge to allow the prisoners to breathe, but it set hard enough to stop them escaping. It was also so sticky that if a prisoner did manage to move, they would stick hard to the first thing they bumped into.

All across Shangrila Lakes there were voices calling out for help, but of course there was no one to help them except the Floods children, who were carrying giant water pistols filled with a special dissolving fluid.

The first person they freed was Anorexya's brother, the gorgeous yet staggeringly stupid Prince Bert Creak.[54]

'Where is your sister?' said Betty.

'Have I got a sister?' said Prince Bert. 'I like your shoes. Hello, shoes.'

'Yes, you have got a sister,' Betty snapped. 'Now, where is she?'

'Um, er. Oh, wait a minute. I have got a sister and she is called Princess Chocolate,' said Prince Bert.

---

[54] *See* The Amazing Illustrated Floodsopedia.

'No, not her,' said Betty. 'She's your nice sister. You've got one that's older than her.'

In the end, they unstuck his mother, Queen Anaglypta Creak, who at first tried to pretend she only had two children.

'Look,' said Mordonna, 'we know you have another daughter and her name's Anorexya. She kidnapped my husband and we need to find her.'

'She was banished from here years ago for unspeakable naughtiness,' said Anaglypta.

'Yes, and now she's back,' said Mordonna. 'I think it would be a good idea for you to help us find her, because I think she's planning to kill you, your husband and your son and then put herself on the Shangrila Lakes throne with my husband at her side.'

Anaglypta said she found that impossible to believe, but when Betty showed her Anorexya's text messages she changed her mind.

'She used to have a secluded cottage at the far end of the lake,' she said. 'If she has come back here, I guess that's where she would be.'

'Right,' said Mordonna. 'In the meantime, I suggest you, your husband and son go somewhere safe to hide, just in case she comes after you.'

The Floods boarded the school bus and skimmed across the lake to Anorexya's cottage, and

there, stuck upside down to the ceiling with porridge, was Nerlin.

After they had released him, they sat the poor enchanted King in a chair and Winchflat erased his brain with a huge electromagnet, before rebooting him from a backup he had on a USB stick.

'I had the strangest dream,' said Nerlin, as one by one the lights inside his head came back on again.

No one had the heart to tell him that the dream hadn't actually been a dream, but a powerful enchantment.

'And Geoffrey-Geoffrey?' said Nerlin. 'Is he part of the dream, or is he real?'

'I'm afraid he's real and he most certainly is not your friend,' Mordonna explained. 'He's very evil and we have to deal with him as soon as we return to Transylvania Waters.'

'What about her?' said Betty, pointing at Anorexya. 'What are we going to do with her, Mother?'

The evil princess was still imprisoned in her porridge coating. When the Floods had arrived she

had used all her strength to try and escape and was now stuck solid halfway in and halfway out of the window. She had managed to free her mouth just enough to let it pour out every single rude word that had ever existed and quite a few new ones that she made up as she went along.

'Well, first of all we'll remove her magic,' said Winchflat.

'Might be a good idea to close her mouth first,' Betty suggested, which – considering Anorexya's swear words were now so strong that large cracks were beginning to appear in the walls – was an excellent suggestion.

With her mouth stuck shut, Anorexya grew redder and redder as the swear words built up inside her. Her entire body grew fatter and fatter. Her clothes split and the thousands of wrinkles in her ancient old body filled out like a hot-air balloon being inflated, but still Anorexya kept on swearing.

'Run for it!' Betty shouted.

She grabbed her father's hand and dragged him outside, and they were followed by the others. As

the Floods ran down to the water's edge, Anorexya exploded.

Bits of skin and fat flew everywhere. A flying elbow smashed into Betty and threw her into the lake. A knee knocked Mordonna's hat off and Anorexya's inside-out left buttock hit Winchflat in the face. Everyone leapt into the lake, where Betty was splashing around washing Old Crone blood and fat out of her hair.

'At least that's solved the problem of what to do with Anorexya,' said Mordonna, after everyone had washed and dried themselves.

Just to make sure Anorexya couldn't re-form herself, Mordonna called a family of vultures down to take away whatever was left of the exploded princess.

Before they left Anorexya's wrecked home and went back across the lake to Bleak, the little town that was the capital of Shangrila Lakes, Mordonna sat Nerlin down to establish how much, if any, Doolallyness there actually was inhabiting his brain.

'How many fingers am I holding up?' she asked him.

'Up what?' Nerlin replied.

'Who is the prime minister?' Mordonna asked.

'Me, of course,' said Nerlin.

'Do you know what day of the week it is?'

'Of course not,' said Nerlin. 'I am the King of the wizards, I have servants to handle that sort of thing.'

'Who is Geoffrey-Geoffrey?'

'I haven't the faintest idea.'

'And finally,' Mordonna said, 'who do you love more than anyone else in the whole world?'

'You, of course, my darling,' said Nerlin with a happy smile.

When Mordonna had told the Creaks that Anorexya was planning to kill them all, the family had hidden in the cellars, except for Prince Bert, who had gone and hidden under his bed.

'I think,' said Mordonna, 'that our two glorious families, the Floods and the Creaks, should form an alliance and see a lot more of each other to stop this sort of thing happening again.'

'Indeed,' said King Marmite Creak, who sort of had a vague thought that maybe, perhaps, there might possibly be a kind of possibility that Princess Betty Flood and Prince Bert Creak might, perhaps, kind of, maybe, possibly, sort of fall in love – preferably with each other – and end up getting married. After

all, a true Floods princess was a far better bet than a princess who had once been a frog.[55]

This thought had actually spent a little time in Mordonna's mind too, though she had dismissed it due to Betty's great intelligence and Prince Bert's great stupidity.

This thought had also spent time in Betty's mind, as she had fallen head over heels in love with the prince as soon as she had seen him on account of him being incredibly handsome and gorgeous. She a witch, he a prince – they were on the same level class-wise.

But then Prince Bert had spoken to Betty, and all her dreams of happiness had come crashing down like an old lady's knickers with broken elastic. Now they lay in a crumpled heap at her feet.

Winchflat noticed how sad his little sister had become, and when she had told him why, he said that when things seemed too good to be true, they usually are.

'All that glitters is not gold,' he said.

---

[55] *See* The Amazing Illustrated Floodsopedia.

Betty nodded in depressed agreement.

'Unless,' Winchflat said with a smile, 'you are a wizard.'

'Whatever,' Betty mumbled.

'If you are a human and are stupid, like most humans are,' Winchflat continued, 'then you are stupid forever. Right?'

Betty nodded.

'But if you are a wizard and are stupid, which very few wizards are,' said Winchflat, 'then something can be done about it.'

Winchflat explained that as well as the traditional Cleverness Spells that could be used to enhance a wizard's talents, he had created a Very Clever Hat, which could be programmed to make its wearer as intelligent as the person giving the hat wanted them to be.

'So, first of all, I would put the Very Clever Hat on you and it would measure your cleverness and intelligence. Then we would put it on Prince Bert and it would program his brain to be five points less clever than you.'

'Wow,' said Betty.

'Or five points more intelligent, if you wanted,' said Winchflat.

'No, I think I like the five-points-less option better,' said Betty.

Before taking the dragon school bus back to Transylvania Waters to get a Very Clever Hat, Winchflat launched a series of Hover Sprays that criss-crossed Shangrila Lakes dissolving all the porridge.

Having seen what Prince Bert was like, Betty decorated the hat with daisies and jelly babies. Then she went upstairs to the prince's bedroom, where he was still hiding under the bed having a conversation with his slippers. He had been asking the slippers if they wanted to go for a walk in the garden and he was a bit upset that they wouldn't answer him.

'I would like to go for a walk in the garden,' said Betty, kneeling down and peering under the bed.

'Hello, pretty lady,' said Prince Bert.

'Hello, pretty prince,' said Betty. 'Would you

like to come for a walk with me? I've got the most wonderful hat you can wear.'

'I like hats,' said Prince Bert. 'But I can't come out because Mummy said my evil sister was going to come and hurt me and make me dead.'

'You don't have to worry about that anymore,' said Betty. 'Your mummy sent me to tell you that your evil sister has exploded and it's safe to come out now. And to come down now, because it's tea time.'

'What day is it?' Prince Bert asked.

'Thursday. Why?'

'On Thursdays we have orange cake for tea,' said Bert. 'I don't like orange cake very much. Couldn't I stay here until Friday, when it's chocolate cake day?'

'Well, I'll tell you what,' said Betty. 'Why don't you come out, put on this lovely hat that I've brought you, and then we could go for a walk by the lake, and if we walked really slowly, by the time we get back it will be Friday and we could have chocolate cake.'

OK,' said the prince. 'Bye, bye, slippers, see you later.'

He wriggled out from under the bed and

whispered to Betty that he had decided he would no longer speak to his slippers because they'd been so rude and he wouldn't be seeing them later either.

'When we go downstairs,' he said, 'I'm going to ask someone to take the slippers and put them in the dustbin. That will teach them.'

Then he saw the hat in Betty's hands. 'Oh, wow!' he said. 'That is the most beautiful hat I have ever seen.'

He took it from Betty and put it on.

Then he stood perfectly still while every single expression it is possible to have moved in an orderly fashion across his face. And hundreds and hundreds of tiny doors inside his brain opened for the first time.

Five minutes later the transformation was complete.

Prince Bert, the most handsome wizard in the world, was now full of incredible cleverness, nearly, but not quite as full as Betty was.

He took Betty's hand and stared deeply into her eyes, making her feel weak at the knees.

'Hello, beautiful lady,' he said in a voice that was now as handsome as the rest of him. 'If I were to ask you to walk beside me by the lake, what would your answer be?'

Betty's knees got so weak it was all she could do to stay standing up.

'My answer,' she began, 'my answer would be, well, um, er, well, all right then, but only for the rest of our lives.'

The two lovers left the castle, drifted hand in hand through the town and walked right around the entire lake very slowly, only stopping seven hundred and fifteen times to kiss each other. This took so long that by the time they got back to the castle, Friday with chocolate cake had become Saturday with strawberry tarts, which only goes to show that even when life seems perfect, there will always be some tiny little thing that's not quite right.

'It's all right, darling,' said Queen Anaglypta to her son. 'I saved you a big slice of Friday's chocolate cake.'

The scene was almost set for everyone to live happily ever after. In fact, quite a few people had already started doing so.

A lot of people had the nagging feeling that something wasn't quite right, though they couldn't put their finger on it. Gruinard could and did put her finger on it.

'And what about Geoffrey-Geoffrey?' she said. Gruinard had stayed and waited at Castle Twilight while the Floods had gone off to Shangrila Lakes.

'Where is he?' Mordonna asked.

'According to our tracking device,' Gruinard said, 'he is on a remote rock called . . .'

'Don't tell me,' said Nerlin. 'Rockall.'

215

'Yes, my lord,' Gruinard replied. 'How do you know of such an insignificant and remote place?'

Nerlin explained that Rockall was where he had banished the evil ex-King Quatorze and Countess Slab, and that only last week he had sent a hailstorm there made of the minced-up frozen remains of the Hearse Whisperer.

'So when Geoffrey-Geoffrey arrived there, it was raining his mother?' said Mordonna.

'It would appear so,' said Nerlin.

'If he is only half as evil as his mother, he will probably have collected enough of her to recreate her,' said Mordonna.

Gruinard was flown by turbo broomstick to her remote valley, where she raced down to her controls and turned on the tracking device.

'He has re-entered the drain and is nearing the coast of Scotland,' she reported down to the castle.

'Then we must act immediately,' said Nerlin. 'We have to block the drain, seal it shut with something that no one will ever be able to remove.'

'In the meantime,' Winchflat said, 'I'll organise

216

a flush-through of a radioactive senna-pod[56] mucus cocktail. It won't stop them, but it will make them very uncomfortable and at least slow them down. Then I'll flush down what they will think is a gentle cleansing fluid to wash out the drain but will actually be nitro-glycerine syrup, which will hopefully blast them into millions of tiny little bits, and even if they don't drink the syrup, it will still explode all around them.'

'Do you really think they'll fall for that?' said Mordonna.

'Doesn't really matter whether they do or not,' said Winchflat. 'If they turn and run for it back to Rockall, they've got no chance of outrunning the flushes.'

---

[56] *When I was a boy, my stepfather used to boil up things called senna pods, drink the disgusting liquid and then spend many happy hours on the lavatory doing various things, which included very complicated crossword puzzles.*

217

'Stop,' said the Hearse Whisperer. 'I think I can hear something.'

'Sorry,' said Geoffrey-Geoffrey, 'it must have been those decomposing seagulls I had for breakfast.'

'No, not that,' said the Hearse Whisperer. 'I said hear, not smell.'

Geoffrey-Geoffrey tilted his head to one side and concentrated.

'Do you mean that very faint roaring noise that sounds like a massive amount of liquid coming down towards us, all the time getting louder and louder?' Geoffrey-Geoffrey said after a while.

'Oh no,' said the Hearse Whisperer. 'I meant the gentle song of skylarks. Of course, I meant the roaring noise, you idiot!'

The noise had changed from very faint to faint, and was now on the verge of beginning to be quite loud.

Without making a noise, the Hearse Whisperer tried to turn and run towards Rockall, but Geoffrey-Geoffrey was perfectly aware of what

his mother was doing and ran after her.

The drain, being very narrow, hacked out of rock and in total darkness, was probably the worst type of place to try to run in. The two of them kept smashing into jagged bits, slipping and tripping and falling over each other. Bleeding, bruised and cursing, they progressed slowly and most definitely a lot slower than the noise, which had now become very loud followed by almost silent as the liquid enveloped the Hearse Whisperer and her son and carried them down the drain at an increasingly rapid rate.

Every now and then one of them stuck their head above the water, just long enough for them to take a breath before being thrown back into the torrent. There was nothing to grab hold of, and besides they had no way of knowing how much liquid there was still behind them.

And then salvation appeared.

A light sparkled through the mucus, getting bigger and brighter as mother and son were carried towards it. It was the end of the drain. The two drowning villains tore and clawed at each other to

try to reach freedom first, which was very stupid and would lead to their downfall.

As they reached the opening they were side by side, arms and legs all tangled together, and they only realised, when it was too late, that the gap was barely wide enough for one of them.

Their heads both went through but no more. The massive force of five million litres of radioactive senna-pod mucus wedged them immovably in the opening.

The Hearse Whisperer tried tearing her son's skin off, but her arms were pinned so tightly that all she managed to do was break her fingernails on her own hip bones. Geoffrey-Geoffrey tried ripping his mother's arms off, but only succeeded in tying their four arms together in a very complicated knot that most boy scouts never even learn.

Meanwhile, back in Transylvania Waters, the Fruit-Pulp Pool had sent down the last of the radioactive senna-pod mucus and Winchflat's team was now carefully pouring the highly explosive nitro-glycerine syrup into the drain. This was followed by a small remote-control device and then finally hundreds of tonnes of quick-set concrete.

'Because we do not want any bits of the Hearse Whisperer or her son backfiring up here,' Winchflat explained.

Winchflat explained that when he set off the

remote-control device, it would explode the nitro-glycerine, killing Geoffrey-Geoffrey and the Hearse Whisperer and blasting their atoms out of the drain and into the icy cold Atlantic Ocean. The trouble was that the tracking device inside Geoffrey-Geoffrey was only accurate to within a hundred metres, so it showed that he was somewhere near Rockall. It did not show that he and his mother were jammed in the drain outlet on the island.

Everyone had a cup of tea and a biscuit while the quick-set concrete set as quickly as it could.

'OK, said Winchflat, checking his watch, 'who would like the honour of pressing the button?'

'I think it should be your father,' said Mordonna, 'considering what he's been through.'

17

There was a VERY, VERY loud

BANG

CUCKOO

18

... which was heard all around the world.

The bang was followed by an almost invisible very, very thin layer of dust, which Winchflat's Micro Dust Analyser analysed as:

- *Ex-King Quatorze – 5%*
- *Countess Slab – 13%*
- *The Hearse Whisperer – 3%*
- *Geoffrey-Geoffrey – 3%*
- *Seagulls (various types) – 0.001%*
- *Seaweed – 0.02%*
- *The sea – 17.5%*
- *Rockall – 58%*

'What about the 0.479%?' said Betty. 'What is that?'

'Probably bacon dust,' said Winchflat. 'The atmosphere's full of it.'

So, not only had the Hearse Whisperer and Geoffrey-Geoffrey been totally and forever obliterated, but so had Ex-King Quatorze, Countess Slab, several assorted seagulls and winkles[57] and the remote island of Rockall.

'A win–win situation all round, really,' said Mordonna.

Everyone agreed, apart from three gannets who had been out sea-fishing and were wondering where on earth their home had gone.

'Probably something to do with global warming,' they said.

---

[57] *Stop sniggering, they are a type of shellfish.*

So finally the scene *was* set for everyone to live happily ever after.

Betty and Prince Bert mooned around holding hands and looking soppy, while in Castle Twilight's main courtyard the Floods and the Creaks – who had come over from Shangrila Lakes to celebrate the reuniting of the two families after years and years of not speaking to each other over some silly argument no one could remember, which had involved a one-legged parrot, three oranges and a cartridge in a pear tree – had a party.

Betty was not the only one of Mordonna and Nerlin's children to fall in love that day. By an amazing coincidence, the Creaks' youngest child,

Tristram Jolyon De-Vere Creak – the Creaks couldn't help themselves, they had a terrible weakness for silly posh names[58] – had been born on Tristan da Cunha in exactly the same hut as Satanella. And as luck would have it, the midwife had used the very same faulty wand that Satanella's grandmother, Queen Scratchrot, had used. Also, coming from a generation that had been brought up to never waste food, the midwife had used a very old prawn that had been lying under the chair.

So it was that Tristram Jolyon De-Vere Creak ended up like Satanella, that is to say, a small dog. Where Satanella had black, wiry fur, Tristram Jolyon De-Vere Creak had golden, silky fur. It was love at first sniff, and as Queen Scratchrot, who had been dug up for the party, said – destiny.

'All that remains now,' said Nerlin, as he and Mordonna sat atop Castle Twilight's tallest tower, sipping their warm blood slurpies and watching the moonlight grovel miserably across Lake Tarnish,

---

[58] *Prince Bert's full name was Prince Bertram Circumstance Augmentation.*

227

'is to sort out who is going to be the next ruler of this wonderful land.'

'Ah, well,' said Mordonna, 'that is another story.'

THE END
For now.

HAVE YOU SEEN THIS BOOK?

THE AMAZING ILLUSTRATED FLOODSOPEDIA

Colin Thompson

Winchflat's Wonderful World of Inventions

Family Fun with Mildew, Germs & Boils

FLOOD FAMILY FRIENDS AND RELATIONS

NERLIN FLOOD'S BEST RECIPE

DISCOVER WHY CATS ARE EVIL & HATE YOU.

WARNING
STANDING ON THIS BOOK WILL MAKE YOU TALLER
SEEK MEDICAL ADVICE BEFORE DOING SO

IF NOT WHY NOT?

POPULAR TREATMENTS FROM THE CRONES' BOOK OF MEDICINE

MAGGOTS: If you are suffering from maggots, dig them out of their hiding places with a warm spoon then serve them on toast with the topping of your choice. Make sure to check behind your knees and in your navel.

TOAST: If you are suffering from an outbreak of toast, immerse yourself in a hot bath. When the toast is nice and soggy, go and lie naked in the garden and wait. Soon, flocks of birds will come and eat the damp bread. Make sure to turn over after about ten minutes so that no stray crumbs are left behind. If there are no birds, you can always use a puppy.

PECKING WOUNDS: If you are covered all over in little holes from the birds' beaks you got from lying covered in wet bread in the garden, you are an idiot for doing it in the first place. What do we learn from this? Always listen to your mum when she tells you to eat your crusts and stop hiding them in your armpits or behind your knees.

TADPOLES: There is NO cure for tadpoles. You're on your own, which is the best thing for someone covered in tadpoles.

GERMY OLIVE

Most people know what 'BOIL' means, but there is another meaning that is completely different. A BOIL is a really gross pimple. These boils are huge and gross and filled with tons of revolting yellow pus. These are the types of boils that Germy Olive uses in her coooking, and if you think that is gross, you should see the other ingredients. If I told you about them, you would throw up all over this book and we wouldn't want that, would we?

Actually, it could be quite good because you'd have to buy another copy.

ANTOINE DE-VEIN GRAND BLOODMASTER

When it comes to blood, Antoine is the world's greatest chef. There is nothing he cannot create from a bucket of blood of any species or vintage - not just food, but cute kittens and even clothes, including the famous blunderpants worn by the Transylvanian Superstar Bram Pit in the film *From Here to Insanity*.

Hush, little baby, don't you cry
Or Mummy will bake you in a pie . . .

Rock-a-bye Baby on the tree top
When the wind blows you will fall off
The branches will break and land on your head
But it won't hurt because you'll be dead.

Baa, baa, Bleak Sheep
Have you any, um, er, wool?
I don't want to talk about it.

Baa, baa, Blank Sheet
Have you any words?
No, they all got eaten
By some angry birds . . .

On the first day of Christmas
My true love gave to me
A pair of big pants
And a slightly used lavatory.
On the second day of Christmas
My true love gave to me
Two morbid goats
And a jam jar full of dragon's wee.

Jack and Jill
Went up the hill
But when they reached the
They both forgot to st
And fell off.

Four and twenty blackbirds baked in a
What a nasty way to make those poor bir

Three blind mice, see how they run
straight into the pussy cat with his great big gun

You need to get it immediately because it is impossible for you to ever realise just what a MASSIVE honour it is for you to have this book. Although Queen Scratchrot warned that it would end in tears, because they are the kindest, greatest wizards who have EVER lived, the Floods have decided to share their immense wisdomness, magic bacon-orientated secrets and history with you, even though you are mere, pathetic humans. Of course, they realise that even though you are mere, pathetic humans, lots of this book will be much too full of cleverness for you to understand, and by no means should you use this book without supervision and extremely strong pants.

JUST BY BEING IN THE SAME ROOM AS THIS BOOK, YOU WILL BE INSTANTLY CURED OF ALL DOOLALLYNESS AND FILLED WITH CLEVERNESS, BIO-DYNAMIC OZONE AND BACON.
JUST ASK YOURSELF — HOW MANY OTHER BOOKS COULD MAKE A PROMISE LIKE THAT?

AMAZING EXCLUSIVE OFFER ONLY AVAILABLE TO PEOPLE WITH A MONEY!! Buy THE AMAZING ILLUSTRATED FLOODSOPEDIA before the end of the months and get ALL the free air you can breather for the rest of your life!!

So, do you think
there might be
a FLOODS app
coming sometime
around Easter?
I know I do.

Probably time to start saving or pestering for an iPad.*

* *Actually, even without a FLOODS app, you really need one.*